BLOODY SEOUL

BY SONIA PATEL

Cinco
Puntos
Press

• EL PASO, TEXAS •

FIRST EDITION
10 9 8 7 6 5 4 3 2 1

Library of Congress Cataloging-in-Publication Data

Names: Patel, Sonia, author.
Title: Bloody Seoul / by Sonia Patel.
Description: First edition. | El Paso, Texas : Cinco Puntos Press, [2019] |
   Summary: Supremely loyal, sixteen-year-old Rocky expects to take over his father's notorious gang, Three Star Pa, one day but after catching his father in a lie, discovers they are not as alike as he believed.
Identifiers: LCCN 2018038398| ISBN 978-1-947627-20-8 (hbk. : alk. paper)
ISBN 978-1-947627-21-5 (pbk. : alk. paper)
ISBN 978-1-947627-22-2 (e-book)
Subjects: | CYAC: Conduct of life--Fiction. | Loyalty—Fiction. | Fathers and sons—Fiction. | Gangs—Fiction. | Bullying—Fiction. | Seoul (Korea)—Fiction. | Korea—Fiction.
Classification: LCC PZ7.1.P377 Blo 2019 | DDC [Fic]--dc23
LC record available at https://lccn.loc.gov/2018038398

Cover and interior art by Zeke Peňa
Book design by Rogelio Lozano / Loco Workshop

FOR MAYA AND JOAQUIN

1.

There are times when I just have to walk.

Not stroll. Not stride.

Just walk—walk the crowded streets of Seoul.

Today I went out again, I had to. It was right after supplemental class ended. 5:59 p.m.

My boys had wanted to hang out at the internet café, hit up some first years for all their money. *Come on, boss, let's do this.*

Not today, I said and turned away. I started walking, hands in my pockets. Time slowed.

I crossed the campus courtyard. A bright tiny bird was perched on a ginkgo tree, singing a wild song. Its crazy melody drowned out the popular girls gossiping in a tight huddle under the shade of the tree's branches. I passed by, turning my head back to catch one more glimpse of this gorgeous flash of yellow. The bird cocked its head to the right, one eye glaring at me.

The popular girls stopped their chatter and stared at me too. Clink of bracelets and some giddy exhales as they turned in my direction.

Cheeks flushed in delicate splotches. Hungry eyes stretched, reaching for a bite of my shoulders, my back.

I came to the school gate, breathed in spring the way I used to breathe in my mother's jasmine perfume. Then my soles hit the city sidewalk. I did a little slouch before I disappeared into the busy line of pedestrians.

It was almost twilight. The sun was already going down between the tall buildings. Charcoal gray clouds dotted the orange, pink, and purple of the sunset.

My mind was feasting on sounds and images. A rain of cherry blossom petals, the skyscraper forest, the rustle of papers being blown along, the distant laughter of children, the hum of car engines.

I wove through the people all stealth, not bumping anyone or anything.

Up ahead—the three towers of the Raemian Caelitus, luxury residential skyscrapers that overlook the Han River. One of them is the thirteenth tallest building in Seoul.

Yeah? And so?

I crossed the intersection. There were three buildings on my right, two regular and one high rise. On the next block, it was just red brick buildings. Six on the right, six on the left. Same number, even number.

Perfect. Nice.

The next section of sidewalk was broken. I stepped between the cracks, thinking about English class. *Step on a crack, break your mother's back.* Don't want to do that, right?

An old woman with gray hair is shuffling slowly in front of me. A few wisps of hair are out of place on one side of her head. She's bent over at the waist and sways a bit with each step. On her next step, her shoe scrapes the sidewalk and she stumbles. I move forward quick, grab her shoulders, hold her upright. I wait until she regains her balance before I let go.

She totters around to face me with an unhurried, gummy smile that intensifies all her wrinkles. Cataracts cloud her eyes, but gratitude cuts through the milky lenses. "You're an angel," she says, pointing at me with her crooked finger.

She reaches for my hand. "Thank you," she says when she gets a hold of it. She flips it over to pat the back. Her eyes get stuck on a ferocious black tiger surrounded by flames, its eyes glowing orange. That's my right hand. She peeks at my left where the head of the fierce red dragon is breathing fire on a black heart. She looks back at me, her smile gone. She backs away, then takes cautious steps to turn around, hobbles off.

My right hand drifts to my belt, to the sheath where I keep my knife. I wrap my fingers around its heavy stainless steel handle. My index finger traces each of the three stars carved into it.

I get back to walking, breathing in and out, keeping track.

I end up at the Han. I always end up at the Han. A different part, but always this river.

On my left is the Banpo Bridge. It pierces the twinkling skyline while the lazy river lies under it almost still, like a sleeping sea snake. There's no one else nearby. Just the way I like it.

The tips of my loafers touch the bottom rail of a metal fence. On the other side, a thin border of overgrown grass and wildflowers. I peer over the vegetation at the Han below. It sloshes, whispering a watery lullaby.

It's time for my kind of nightcap. I take my Dunhill International cigarette tin from my jacket, the one I've had since I was six. It was my mom's. I didn't fill it with Dunhills until two years ago when I started smoking. I've tried other brands but Dunhill is the best. I prefer its slower burn, gives me more time to enjoy the spicy sweetness of the tobacco. More time to think, to remember.

Inside the tin is my parents' old wedding photo. It fits perfectly inside the lid.

My mother is so beautiful. She's smiling the way she used to smile at me. A news guy on TV once said she was the country's most promising ingénue. A true rising star. I imagined throngs of fans chanting her name. *Gil Bo-young! Gil Bo-young!*

My dad. Yi Dae-sung. My older uncle used to say I'm the spitting image of Dae-sung, his middle brother. Mom said the same thing. She used to stroke my cheek and whisper, "My little Yi Kyung-seok. My little Rocky. Your eyes are icy cold black like your dad's. They make you dangerously handsome, just like him."

She's the one who gave me that nickname. Rocky. "The look on your face never changes. It's steadfast. Like a rock."

I light up, take a few sips until the cherry is established, then a long draw, exhaling a smoky cloud through my mouth and nose. Nice dizzy feeling.

Car horns beep overhead on the bridge. There's a traffic jam on the top tier.

I take one last drag and crush the burning stub on a trashcan.

Behind me, children laugh and squeal. I look over my shoulder. A brother and sister exchange fake scowls. They're holding hands with their grinning parents.

Suddenly I just can't get enough air. I grab at my tie, then at the collar of my white dress shirt. I open my mouth and try to gulp down some oxygen. But the air won't go in.

I quick take off my jacket and tie, pull open the collar of my shirt, busting the top button, and double over.

Finally, I can get a few full breaths.

When I bend down to grab my tie, my father's face is staring back at me from the Han's mirror surface.

Yeah, it's me, not him, and I am the spit image.

I slip out of my dress shirt. My tatted up chest and arms burst out of my undershirt.

I have hardly any untouched skin. Just like my dad. But I'm most proud of my dragon and tiger because they're exactly like his.

My dad's a walking masterpiece. When I was little, I'd climb the step stool in his bathroom. With a towel wrapped around his waist, he'd lean towards the mirror to shave. I'd adjust my towel. Pretend to shave. My precious few minutes to view his vivid koi, warrior, flowers, waves...

I'd frown at my pale yellow-white skin. Plain and boring but with so much potential. Like a sheet of Dad's parchment stationery waiting to be inked. Maybe, I thought, when I grow up I could be a walking masterpiece too.

My reflection copies the slow stroke of my sideburn.

I thump my right fist over each of the three blank spaces across my chest. I'm saving those areas for three black star tattoos. Only Three Star Pa members are allowed that signature ink.

My dad won't let me talk about gang stuff yet, though, not until I'm done with university.

But I've got my own plans.

Whether my dad likes it or not, I'm going to take over TSP ASAP. I will be the big boss sooner rather than later.

My mom didn't want me to have anything to do with Three Star Pa.

Well, she's not around to stop me, is she?

2.

So high up should only be for gods. On second thought, people talk to Dad like he's a god, one they fear. An angry, vengeful god. Maybe we do belong in our penthouse that's closer to the clouds than any other top floor in Hongdae.

Raindrops pop on the tiled edge of the balcony.

I sink deeper in the loveseat, cradling my small ceramic bowl. I take two quick sips of the sweet, tart, and creamy makgeolli, then make one vigorous swirl. The tiny, milky whirlpool of liquor looks like today's weather in a bowl.

Dad's bowl is empty. He downed it before he went inside to answer a call.

The ethereal clouds continue to sprinkle their blessed holy water. The city below is cloaked in a thick gauzy veil of fog.

I breathe in a deep, long stretch of heavy air. Can I inhale all the fog?

It suddenly lifts.

Deep breath, fog's death. English class. My way.

The light rain stops too.

I rest my head on the back cushion and close my eyes. *Nessun Dorma* shrouds me in its sound, a sad richness that descends like an operatic fog. The two Spaniards go first—Plácido Domingo followed closely by José Carreras. Then the Italian enters with his solo and my eyes spit out tears. It happens every time. I open my eyes to the heavens crying with me.

How can a voice be so fearless yet so lonely?

I slip my hand in my pocket, clutch my handkerchief. It's super soft, like my fingers are wrapped around a cloud. It's plain and white, but Mom was supposed to embroider it, the way she did for Dad.

She removed the handkerchief from the embroidery hoop. She smoothed the cloth, then held it up. "What do you thi…" she started to ask but stopped when she looked at me. She leaned over and dabbed my wet cheeks with Dad's gift. "Oh, if Pavarotti knew his voice is the only thing that can move my little Rocky."

I liked the way the bumpy stitches of the willow tree kissed my skin.

A few tears run down my chin. The rain starts coming down in sheets. *The heavens are sobbing…*

Dad's penetrating voice interrupts from the other room. I let go of my handkerchief and rip my hand out of my pocket. In nothing flat I wipe my cheeks with the backs of my hands.

"I told you to take it easy on him!" Dad yells.

I look over my shoulder. He's pacing and waving an arm.

Two more sips, a quick swirl, then I set the makgeolli bowl on the table and launch up to the railing. Way down on the street the open umbrellas are like the multi-colored round beads in my old kaleidoscope. I aim a pretend kaleidoscope, the way I used to when I was little, and turn the end of the tube. The pattern shifts as people underneath their umbrellas walk.

Rainy day Seoul. I cross my arms, whip around, and lean against the slick metal bars. The lonely acacia wood loveseat cries out *Why have you forsaken me?* Just like the guy who hands out Jesus pamphlets in the Hapjeong subway station. My mother should be nestled there on the black cushions with my father next to her. They should be drinking their makgeolli and smoking their Dunhills. And me, I should be sitting cross-legged on the cool tile devouring some book. The Onkyo spinning the opera…

But that would have been ten years ago.

Dad barks, "You were only supposed to incapacitate him a bit. I do the rest! You know what this means." The top buttons of his dress shirt are open. He strokes the three stars on the diamond encrusted medallion around his neck. It drags the chunky gold chain down like an angler's line that's hooked a huge Chinese seerfish.

I touch my bare neck, wishing for the weight of precious metal and stone. Only TSP bosses—Dad, Older Uncle, and Younger Uncle—get the chain and medallion.

Does Younger Uncle wear his chain like his ink? I have no idea. All I know is that Dad ousted him from TSP years ago and that we're forbidden to talk about him. Or to him, wherever he is.

Older Uncle always wore his chain, even after he died. The bulky gold draped his portrait like a glistening garland. That is, until Dad caught me trying to pinch it.

Older Uncle's portrait hangs to the left of where Dad's smacking the wall.

Six years ago I pushed a chair in front of his proud smiling face and climbed up. I reached out for his boss gold. My fingers brushed the cold, shiny links. My eyes feasted on the sparkling white gems.

"Rocky!" Dad hollered.

I froze.

"Rocky, look at me!"

I cringed, then turned my head in slow motion over my shoulder.

"NEVER touch that!" He marched over and pushed me off the chair.

My body landed, butt first, on the floor. My head hit an end table, the cracking sound scared me, but I didn't move.

Dad grabbed Older Uncle's chain, medallion first. He shined it with his sleeve. Then he bowed to the portrait and whispered, "I'm sorry Rocky disturbed you, Older Brother. It's my fault. I should've kept this hidden." He stuffed the necklace into his pocket. "Consider it done." He bowed one more time before he whipped his head to me. The muscles in his face tightened. "What?" he growled. "Can't handle a little push?" He shook his head. "Just like your mom. Are you going to run away now too? You want to be with your mom? Good luck finding her." He stared at me hard. "She left us!" he bellowed before he stomped away.

Dad stomps back and forth. "Stupid idiot!" he erupts. He swats an antique pottery vase. It flies across the room, hits the wall, and lands with a crash. One...two...three...four...five...six...seven large shards. And a bunch of little ones...

Older Uncle swept up the big pieces of the porcelain vase.

"I don't know what to do," Mom whispered, touching her cheek that was purple and red.

"Dae-sung's gone too far," Older Uncle mumbled, brushing up the smaller pieces.

"I'm scared he'll..." Mom's voice trailed off. Her eyes grew wide. "And Kyung-seok..."

"Don't worry," Older Uncle said. "I'll talk to boss two. I'll make sure this never happens again. Business is business but family is separate. Family comes first. Family is to be protected at all costs. That's the code. And we didn't make it the first out of seven by coincidence."

I touch my cheek.

Mom was an actress. She stayed in character, kept her makeup on for me sometimes because she knew I liked that. Still...

Did someone hurt my mom?

I've gone over it in my head so many times.

I hear Older Uncle's voice again.

Dae-sung's gone too far...

Did Dad hurt Mom?

Who, Dad? No way! Bury that! I shake my head. He hurts other people, not his family. Never his family. Pushing me off the chair doesn't count. He was just being protective of Older Uncle's necklace. And it's not as if Dad bashed my head onto the table. That was an accident. Dad wouldn't defy the first tenet of the very TSP code he helped establish.

The second tenet is an eye for an eye. Dad likes to talk about that one.

I rest an elbow on the slippery railing and prop my chin, wishing I knew the remaining five tenets. I asked Dad about them once. He scowled, then told me to mind my own business. I frowned inside and walked away, even though I really wanted to say, *But Dad, the gang will be my business one day. I'm the sole heir of TSP, aren't I?*

I flick seven beads of rain. I am the sole heir. Why don't I have the guts to say it to his face?

"Don't do anything else. My knife will take care of him," Dad orders. "It always does what I command, not like you," he tries to mutter but his voice is thundering.

That's why.

Dad does more pacing. "I'll be right over." He shoves his phone into his pocket, his arms into his jacket, and his feet into his Ferragamo's. He rushes out without saying a word to me, slamming the front door behind him.

I jump.

I push my palm onto my chest. My heart pounds it like it's mad at me.

Another smoke. Yes. That's what I need. That and more makgeolli.

I polish off my half bowl and what's left in the bottle. My hand tries to crush the bowl. I can't. So I hurl it across the balcony. It shatters on the tile.

One, two, three, four shards. Unlucky four, the number that in Korean and Japanese sounds like the word for death. Also in Mandarin, according to Mom. I might as well count one, two, three, death...

Tragic four, death for sure.

I peel my eyes away. Light up a Dunhill. Smoke it fast and hard, then crumble the stub in my hand, letting the grainy mess rain into the ashtray. I spring up and march to my room.

I go straight to my armoire, seize my knife from the top shelf. Three quick steps to my designated spot. Aim. Throw. No spin. The knife hits the wooden beam four meters away. It stays stuck, quivering slightly from the force of the impact. I walk the six steps to the beam, take a moment to run my fingers over the hundreds of small cuts already there—years of target practice—then pluck out the knife. The only knife for me. The kind assassins use.

I inspect my knife. I buff out a smudge on the blade with my sleeve.

My knife will take care of him. It always does what I command...

"This knife matches mine. It will always do what you command..." Dad ran his finger over the polished stainless steel blade, "...but you have to be the boss." He lit up a Dunhill, took a long drag, exhaled three rings. "It was made by a craftsman in Busan who specializes in ancient weapons. Go on. Pick it up."

I lifted it. It was heavier than I expected. The blade was almost as long as my six-year-old forearm. I inspected it from all angles. It radiated death. I checked out the handle and my heart fluttered. My name was carved in Hangul on one side, and there were three stars carved on the other.

Smile! Hug him! Hug me back, Dad!

I bowed. "Gamsahamnida," I said, my face straight. I examined my new knife a bit more. I thought about the three black stars tattooed on my father's chest. I asked, "Abeoji, why are there three stars?"

"Ahhhh," he said, stroking my head. "I'll tell you. But it's our family's secret, ok?"

I nod.

"One star for each Yi brother."

Mom's voice. "Let's eat," she called out from the kitchen.

"Coming."

I sliced the air with my knife, then thrust it into the heart of an imaginary foe.

Dad laughed. "Tomorrow we'll go to the park at sunrise. I'll teach you to cut and throw." He lifted my chin. "With practice, you can control any fight. You can hurt someone. Or kill them. It's you, not the knife, that decides."

I watched his lips move, taking it all in. My fingers traced the stars. My thumb traced my name. I traced again, looking at the blade. Does real blood look as watery red as it does in Mom's movies?

He held up the leather box. "But remember, always an eye for an eye. Never more." He motioned for me to put my knife back. I hesitated.

"Tomorrow," he promised with a hard nod.

I placed my knife carefully in the box. He closed it, then returned it to the chest. He walked to the packed bookshelf, gliding his index finger over the spines on the middle shelf. He stopped on an olive-colored one and pulled it out. "Here. Study this tonight. It's the best," he said holding it out. "Learn it well."

I took the book: *The Netter Collection of Medical Illustrations: The Cardiovascular System.* I flipped it open and skimmed a few pages of detailed, colorful illustrations of the inside of the human body. I closed the book, cradled it against my chest.

"You need to know the human body if you want to be a true knife master," my father said. He pointed to the book. "Open it again."

I turned to a random page, to a color drawing with the words "exposure of the heart" printed above it.

"The red blood vessels carry the clean blood to the body, and the blue vessels carry the dirty blood back to the heart, then to the lungs for purification."

I started memorizing. *Aorta. Superior vena cava.*

"You'll understand it better when you read the descriptions."

I looked back at him.

He poked his chin out. "Remember, the red ones are your targets."

Targets. His knife. My knife's twin.

How many red ones has he hit? Will he hit one tonight? More than one?

I'm squeezing the handle so tight that blood can't flow to my hand, it's all white and tingly. I'm breathing faster.

Aim. Throw.

Sixteen times, one for every year of my life.

Aim. Throw.

Ten times, one for every year Mom's been gone.

Aim. Throw.

Ten times, one for every year Dad's been the most pissed off person I've ever known.

3.

The new kid is strong. He twists and kicks as Patch and Strike drag him behind the dumpster. The more the kid struggles, the harder my boys clamp down on his shoulders and arms.

Braid and I saunter behind, hands in our pockets.

Braid kicks a pebble, then looks at me. "Boss?"

I quick check the open end of the alley. There's no one between us and the math building on the other side of the long, parallel rows of intense pink cherry blossom trees.

I nod.

Braid half smiles. His waist length, tight braid whips the air when he turns to the new kid. "The payment is due today, you dumb jock," he says, grabbing a fistful of the kid's hair and yanking his head back. "No less than five hundred thousand won."

Dumb Jock scowls. The ripe pimples on his face bulge. "I don't have it," he spews. He curls his upper lip. "As if you rich boys need it," he mutters.

Braid lets go of DJ's hair. He jogs to the other side of the dumpster, then marches back, slapping DJ's baseball bat onto his open palm.

"Not his face or hands," I say before I light up a Dunhill. *Not where anyone else will notice.*

Braid nods. He's already in a batting stance. He makes a couple of small circles above his head with the barrel. Then he lets a home run rip, straight into DJ's gut.

DJ wails.

Braid drops the bat. He plows forward and punches DJ in the chest. Then Braid snatches the top of DJ's ear and stretches it. "Listen up, junior boy. Since you're new here, let me spell it out for you. We're your seniors. We run the school. If you don't pay our price, your body pays instead. Got it?"

DJ glares at Braid. "Bring it," he dares. Then he spits. The frothy wad meant for Braid lands on Patch's shiny shoe.

Patch shakes his head, his lips pursed.

Strike chuckles. "You shouldn't have done that." He points to Patch with his chin. "He's gonna—"

DJ cuts him off. "Why don't you let the patch-wearing cyclops speak for himself?"

Strike looks at Patch. With a professorial voice he says, "This loser is also a complete idiot with no real knowledge of classical Greek mythology."

Patch smiles. He clinches DJ's arm extra hard with one hand, then slips the soiled shoe off with the other. He shoves it in DJ's face.

"Put your spit back in your mouth, jackass," Strike orders.

DJ turns his head away.

Braid slithers behind DJ. "Do it!" he yells, his plier hands forcing DJ's face to the shoe.

DJ seals his lips.

Strike knees DJ's flank.

DJ grimaces but presses his lips together even more.

Patch mashes the spit-covered toe cap onto DJ's lips.

"Do it now!" Braid shouts.

DJ's lips part slowly. He licks the shoe clean.

Then Patch wipes his shoe on DJ's sleeve before he slides it back on.

Strike smiles at DJ. "That wasn't so hard now, was it? And for your information," he says, "my buddy here has two eyes. He just wrecked one doing a noble deed. And why should he throw away perfectly good words on the likes of you? But you wouldn't understand any of that, you pathetic waste of space who doesn't deserve the two working eyes and vocal cords he has."

Patch grins, then knees DJ's opposite flank.

DJ grunts.

I smile inside. *Both flanks. Even is good.* I take a full draw on my cig, hold it in my mouth. The woody, peppery, sweet mint flavors fuse. I release three smoke rings, one for each of my mini Three Star Pa school gang. I stare at DJ. Another drag. The gentle heat embraces my lungs. I exhale through the side of my mouth. The smoke coils up.

Braid looks at me. "What should we do with him, boss?"

"Yeah, boss," DJ chimes in, "What should they do with me?" He gives a sly smile. "Can't be worse than what I did with your mom," he says.

My face stays blank. No comeback. Yet. I let my cig dangle from my lips. My hand drops to my knife, my fingers waltz over my stars, my name.

DJ licks his lips. "Your mom was delicious," he says in a smoky voice.

Cool face. Hot inside. My heart pumps boiling blood. Without warning I stub out my cig on DJ's arm, mashing it into his flesh good and hard so he'll have something to remember this day. He jerks his body and contorts his face as the cigarette burns, but he doesn't let out the scream I know wants to escape.

I drop the cigarette butt and extract my knife in a perfect flow that takes three seconds because I make it take three seconds. I slice the air with the shiny blade. I look at Braid. "Hold his mouth open," I command.

DJ's face contorts. He clenches his mouth.

Braid pries DJ's lips and teeth apart.

I make my blade dance a little. Then I skim the tip over my cheek, keeping my eyes on DJ. "Didn't your parents teach you any manners?" I ask.

DJ's eyebrows bump together. He moans. He squirms, but my boys tighten their hold.

"I guess I'll have to teach you," I say. My left hand captures his tongue. "Lesson number one, never speak about anyone's mother." I touch the flat side of the blade to the tip of his tongue.

DJ gets all bug-eyed.

My boys laugh.

DJ shuts his eyes, a few tears leak out the corners. A wet patch spreads on the front of his trousers.

Then, just like that, I holster my knife.

Braid lets go of DJ's mouth.

"Have the money to us within the hour," I say.

DJ nods vigorously, sweat dripping.

I chin up to my boys. They close in. They finish the lesson the old fashioned way—corporal punishment.

Meanwhile I lean up against the wall for another smoke. I light up and hold the cig close to my body in between drags.

Out of the corner of my eye, a flash of red at the alley's open end. I turn my head. A guy in a black suit with a red pocket square darts by. He disappears before I get a clear look at his face.

It couldn't be a student. Pocket squares are not part of our uniforms. Was it some random guy passing by with a red pocket square? Perhaps. But unlikely on our school campus.

I take slow draw on my cig, sucking the smoke deep into my lungs. I hold it there.

Or, Chul-moo? Or Braid's older cousin, In-su?

Maybe. The privilege of wearing red pocket squares was bestowed on those two TSP guys—and those two TSP guys alone—by my dad. See, they're higher ups in TSP. My dad's most trusted men.

But why would either of them be here?

I look again. This time, nothing. No one. I release a billowy cloud.

Shrug inside. *Doesn't matter.*

4.

The noise of smashing and shattering wakes me up like a punch to the groin. I bolt up, all my senses on high alert. My clock trumpets the time in blood red. **1:05 a.m.** But besides my heavy breathing and thumping heart, there is only silence, a strange stillness. I push the covers back, slink out of bed, and sneak into the living room. All the lights are on. Dad's slumped over on the sofa, an empty whiskey bottle in one hand and his knife in the other.

Broken glass and black wood fragments litter the coffee table and surrounding floor. I take a few cautious steps, but then a bright flash immobilizes me. Lightening cuts the sky in the distance, brilliant zigzags on a coal background. I hold my breath.

Thunder booms loud enough to make me shudder.

I exhale and move toward my father, tiptoeing around the pieces of glass that seem to be from the tabletop photo frame that lays broken on the floor. The photo is cut in two unequal halves. It was of the three of us, the only family photo we had on display, but Dad sliced my mother out of it.

I pick up Mom's half, then I retrieve Dad and me. I lay both halves on the coffee table. Stare at them, palms to my forehead, fingers splayed.

Yeah, Dad's been wasted and awful plenty of times before, but this... how could he do this? And with his knife?

That's not what your knife is for, Dad. That's not what you taught me. How could you let your knife be so cruel? What about the first tenet of the TSP code?

Maybe he was following the second tenet.

Mom left us, cut us out of her life, so shouldn't we cut her out of ours? An eye for an eye.

I shake my head. No. I don't like that. But maybe he just really misses her. Like I do.

I take the knife out of his hand, put it on the table. Then I pry his fingers off the empty whiskey bottle, set it next to his knife, and lower his torso onto the leather cushions. Slide a pillow under his sweaty head. His legs are deadweight when I swing them onto the opposite end. I drape his arms over his gut. He looks like he's in a cremation casket. *Bad luck.* I roll him on his side, towards me. *Better.* And this way he won't choke if he pukes.

Back to the debris. I clean up the glass and wood. Then I carry the two sections of our family photo back to my room, all delicate, like they're ancient scrolls. I fit the bisected edges together. Tape it, front and back.

I prop the photo on a floating shelf that's at eye level. I haven't had a good look at it in awhile. It was taken ten years ago on the Roof Terrace of Namsan Seoul Tower. I look closer. *There it is.* The gochujang red lovelock I'd just fastened to the chain link fence. Our family's lovelock.

I bounded up the last five steps. I wanted to be the first one to lay my eyes on the Roof Terrace's long fence, because I knew when I saw it I'd get the Christmas feeling even though it wasn't December. I loved the Christmas feeling. Warmth and merriment. Candy and raised glasses. Crisp air and cold, red cheeks. Crunchy snow and a crackling fire. Peace and harmony. Love.

I wanted the Christmas feeling first.

Plus the fence reminded me of a flat Christmas tree, the thousands of lovelocks hanging from it like an infinite number of ornaments. Silver. Gold. Solid colors. Sparkly.

I looked over my shoulder. Mom and Dad were climbing hand-in-hand. Talking. Laughing.

My parents are smiling in the photo, and Dad's got his arm around Mom. I'm standing in front of them. They've both got a hand on my shoulders.

"Smile, Rocky," Mom said. She knew I wasn't smiling even without looking.

Why didn't I smile?

I never did. Not even at the best times—Dad's private knife lessons in the park and Mom's weekly haemul pajeon dinners. Not even the one time the best times happened on the same day.

"Dad," I said, "may I please show Mom what you taught me today?" I waited for his answer. I wanted to smile, but I didn't. I focused on the grand spread of homemade banchan on the low table instead. The fiery red, green, and pale yellow of the gimchi…

"Yes, Rocky. Go get your knife."

My eyes widened, but I caught myself. I hadn't thought that he'd say yes. I wanted to leap up and run to his den, but I made myself get up slow and walk. When I came back with the black box, Mom was standing over the table with the large, sizzling cast iron skillet.

Pavarotti's *Mamma* came on.

My mouth watered. My eyes didn't move from the skillet. The familiar, savory aroma made me change my mind about showing her my new knife trick. *After we eat.* I put the box on the floor next to me.

Mom kneeled and set down the skillet in the middle of the table. She took off her mitts, smiling at me. She served Dad first, then me, and then herself.

"I appreciate you preparing this meal," Dad said.

"Thank you for making the food," I said.

Mom and I waited until Dad lifted his chopsticks before we touched ours. We always let him start eating before we dug in. I dipped my first bite in the sauce then delivered the crispy treasure to my mouth. Closed my eyes as I chewed. I couldn't imagine anything tasting better. When I opened my eyes, Mom was looking at me, still smiling.

"There's no one I'd rather make it for than you, Rocky. There's no place I'd rather be than here with you."

I was used to her saying things like that, so I didn't think anything of it. Not until I realized her eyes were filled with tears. I was about to smile back, but then Dad muttered something and flung his spoon which was heaped with rice. It hit the wall behind me and landed with a clang on the floor. He pushed his plate away, shot up, and stomped off.

Mom's smile was gone. She watched Dad until he disappeared into his den. Then she wiped her eyes and looked at me, tried to smile again.

I tried to smile back at her, but I couldn't. My smile stayed inside.

It's stayed inside ever since.

I look at the photo again.

I need to get out of here. Need to walk.

I pat the upper left side of my suit. Dunhill tin—check. Pat my trouser pockets. Lighter, pocket watch, cell phone—check, check, check.

Knife.

I get it from the beam. "I'd never leave you behind," I whisper and slide it gently into its sheath.

I creep to the doorway. Dad's snoring like his fire-breathing dragon tat came alive but had a bad cold.

I scan the rack of expensive shoes. My Ferragamo monk strap loafers call to me. Thick-soled for pounding the concrete. Slip my feet in.

I walk right past the three umbrellas that hang near the door—Dad's black one, Mom's yellow one, and mine is red.

I want to walk *in* the weather. Mom taught me that, she liked weather. So do I. The way it feels on my face. In my hair. In my lungs when I breathe it in.

I pull the door shut behind me and check the doorknob. It's unlocked.

I start down the hallway but stop. I pivot and march back to the door. I turn the knob. It's unlocked. I stuff my hands in my pockets and walk towards the elevator. I'm halfway there but end up turning around a third time. I practically run back to the door to test the knob again. It's still unlocked.

I head out for real this time.

A fast elevator ride to the lobby, my usual nod to the doorman, and my feet plant on the sidewalk. I hold out my palm, it's drizzling. The sky is nothing but mist and black. I don't care. Neither does the city. It's bright and flashy.

I breathe in the damp air. Hands in pockets, head down, I take my first step.

It's crowded. Umbrella spokes graze the shaved sides of my head. Raindrops get lost in my longer hair on top, a few tickle my scalp. My feet splash in puddles. Cars switch on headlights. Windshield wipers swish. Raincoats squeak past each other.

I close my eyes for a second and hear Pavarotti's majestic voice.

I walk and walk and walk. An hour? Two?

I stop only when my next step would be into the Han.

My hand drifts to my chest. My heartbeat is steady, everything is okay.

My cell rings. I check. It's Dad. I ignore it.

Everything is ok.

I waver.

Is everything ok?

Everything is ok. I stand up straight. I nod.

That's right. Everything is ok.

My cell rings again. Dad, again. "Hello?"

"Where are you?" he hollers. "Do you know what time it is? Do you..."

I hold the phone away from my ear as his voice slaps me around.
What the heck? He was out like a light.

"Get your ass home right now or else!" he screams.

"Ok."

When Dad's like this, I do what he says.

When it was the three of us, things were different.

A flash of lightning forks behind all the buildings on the other side of the river.

Why did Mom leave me alone with him?

Thunder grumbles low, then cracks the air.

The next thunder explosion is like a belt. It whips me out of my calm. I flinch then back away from the Han. With the next crash I turn on my heels and run.

This is no time for a slow walk home, the thunder shouts, chasing me.

Fortunately there's a subway station on the next corner. I fly down the steps and leap onto my train just before the doors slide closed.

By the time I get back to the penthouse, my father's pacing in the living room. He's well into another bottle of whiskey and smoking on overdrive. Dunhill butts form the foundation of a tower on the ashtray like Jenga blocks. I shut the front door as quiet as I can, hoping to slip past him to my room.

No such luck.

He sees me. He stops marching and glares at me. He takes a big swig of whiskey. Wobbles. Eyes me for a second then storms towards me.

I hide how scared I am. Gangsters, especially future bosses, aren't supposed to be afraid. I manage to keep my deadpan expression. I pull my shoulders back and push my chest out.

Too bad my sweat betrays me. It leaks out of every pore. It drips into my eyes, but I don't let myself blink or lift a hand to rub it away though it stings.

Dad's in my face now. "Where the fuck were you?" he screams. His hot breath smells like flowers that someone watered with gasoline.

"On a walk," I say in as neutral a voice as possible.

"Did I say you could go on a walk?" he yells. He takes another gulp of whiskey.

"No. I'm sorry," I say, bowing.

"Sorry doesn't cut it," he says then shoves me with one hand.

I stumble backwards. The wall catches me. I straighten up and look at my bedroom door. I need to get to my room. He won't bother me in there. I take slow, sideways steps.

Dad plows toward me, shoves me two more times.

I end up with my back against the wall again.

He unbuckles his belt. "This boy needs a lesson," he mutters under his breath. He tugs on the metal clasp.

My body stiffens. *What about the TSP co—*

Just then his cell rings. He frowns as he lets go of the belt to answer.

I think I'm out of the woods, but he raises the bottle and makes like he's going to smash it into the side of my head.

I duck, my arms shielding my head.

He catches my eye and postures one more time before he walks away, giving angry instructions to whichever TSP guy is on the phone. He disappears into his room. The slamming of his bedroom door makes me jump.

He's done manhandling me it seems, but I can't move. I can't think so I count. It's the only thing I can do.

Sixty-two seconds until I can take my first shaky step.

5.

My boys and I strut to the grand arched entrance of our school's
dining hall. It's well into lunchtime, so the elegant room is jam-packed
with munching and gossiping students. I do my stealthy surveillance,
clockwise. It always has to be clockwise.

At five o'clock is a table of popular girls. Ten gleaming eyes bat at me.
Cupped hands as they loud whisper to each other.

"So handsome."

"My kind of hot bad boy."

I yawn at them, not bothering to cover my mouth. Whatever.
Popular or not, they're like sheep who know they can't get too close to
the wolf. Me. The alpha. And my boys are my betas.

I check the row of chandeliers. The one in the middle is still only half
lit.

Everything's ok then.

My betas and I swagger in, straight to our table at the far back
corner. The best, of course. Our territory, claimed and marked. My boys
wait for me to sit before they do.

I bust out my Dunhills. Light up. The school staff looks the other way, they have to. They know who my dad is.

But I hate that. I'd rather it be because they know who I am—the boss of mini Three Star Pa—and what we've done—earned our status as the rulers of the school.

My dad's not boss here. I am. I'm the king.

I behold my subjects.

The popular girls are still eyeing me.

I do a smoke trick.

"A ghost!" one of them squeals.

They all giggle and their bracelets clink as they cover their mouths. They're so easily amused. So boring.

I look away and turn to Braid. "The Three Tenors," I say.

Braid nods. His eyes and fingers trail down the stack of my favorite opera records. More perks from the school—an Onkyo, speakers, and records. He selects an album near the bottom. I close my eyes so it will be a surprise. The crackling sound when he lays the stylus on the spinning vinyl makes the little hairs on my arms stand. The orchestra starts. Immediately I know which song it is. *Una Furtiva Lagrima.* Haven't heard it in forever. I count the seconds of the long minute until the fearless timbre of my idol fills the room.

An ache of familiarity. I squeeze my eyelids tighter. I see Younger Uncle and Mom in our penthouse. A childhood memory? A half-remembered dream? Younger Uncle pours red wine. Smiles as he hands Mom the stemless glass. She looks away. Sips…

Then the vision is gone. And so is the odd feeling.

I open my eyes. I bask in the lush warmth and depth of analog, something not possible with digital.

Braid laughs at some joke he made about the "seaweed bits" stuck on Strike's chin and upper lip.

Meanwhile Strike sneaks his hand behind Braid. "Ha!" he says, "At least I can grow hair on my face! Not like some people…" He laughs. His fingers wrap around Braid's braid. His laugh transforms into fake moans as he tugs. He jumps up behind Braid. Now he's gyrating his hips. Moaning louder.

Patch holds his belly, cracking up silently.

All of a sudden, Strike freezes. Braid's braid slips out of his hand. He's staring at the entrance. His lips move. "Look who's here, boss," he says, "Black Coolie." He contorts his face.

I look over my shoulder. Sure enough there's Ha-na. All alone, like always, like she should be, because I made it law. In fact, it's the first law I established as boss a few years ago—no one at school can hang out with her. A couple of months later, after a particular world history lesson, I expanded the Ha-na law: everyone has to call her "Black Coolie." The British called their indentured servants from India and China "coolies," but the term turned into a slur. And Ha-na is slur worthy because I say so. Especially when she's on my turf.

Ha-na Desai. She's half-Indian, half-Korean. She pulls more Indian because she's dark brown.

Brown. Black. It's all the same to me—the opposite of light. Maybe I wouldn't be so repulsed by her if she was some other dark and not part Indian.

My mom had a bad encounter with some Indians once. I was there when she told Older Uncle about it. I remember it like it was yesterday because it's the only time I've ever heard Mom complain about anything.

I was almost six. I was supposed to be sleeping. Older Uncle had tucked me in an hour before. But I was wide awake, excited that he was around because my dad never seemed to be home anymore. So I snuck out of my room and hid under one of the end tables in the living room. I played quietly with my toy car. And listened. Watched.

Older Uncle sipped on a cup of tea. "How are you and Dae-sung doing?" he asked.

Mom smiled a nervous smile and looked away. Then, eyes on her feet, she said, "Fine. We're fine."

"Has he—"

Mom whipped her head up. "No!" she blurted. "No. Don't worry. He hasn't done that in awhile."

Older Uncle squinted as he examined Mom's face.

"He hasn't, really. I'd tell you," Mom said with lots of long blinking. I counted the blinks, eight. She took two quick sips of her tea, avoiding Older Uncle's eyes.

Older Uncle nodded. He sat back. "I'm relieved to hear that," he said. He took a sip then asked, "I guess last week was because of something else?"

Mom scratched her neck. "Last week," she began. She touched her mouth before she gave an ill-timed smile. "Oh, yes, last week. Yes, I had a bad migraine." She raised her eyebrows and interlaced her hands. "Glad it's gone. I'm feeling much better."

"Good. That's good," Older Uncle said. He gulped some tea.

Mom sat up straight, a sour expression on her face as if she just took a bite of overly fermented gimchi. "You know what else happened last week?" She wrinkled her nose.

Older Uncle shook his head.

"Some random G.I. slipped me something at the club."

Older Uncle leaned in toward my mother. "Slipped you something?"

Mom didn't answer. She kept going, speaking faster. "Those G.I.s, such rude and arrogant U.S. soldiers, hit on me. They were dark, but not black, Indian maybe? Anyway, one of them tried to kiss me! I held up my left hand, practically shoved my wedding ring in his face. He grabbed my hand and wouldn't let go. He laid a tiny plastic bag in my palm then said, 'You'll want me after this.' Then he winked, and just like that he and his buddy turned to go. But not before I heard one of them say to the other, 'That Dae-sung—I can't believe he got his wife into this shit.'"

Older Uncle frowned. "Dae-sung wouldn't do that. He wouldn't go against the code," he said.

Mom rested her chin on her hand and nodded. "I know," she said, "I didn't believe them."

He lifted an eyebrow. "You didn't try it, did you?" he asked with a hard look.

She had trouble meeting his gaze. She looked down and away. "Of course not," she whispered.

"And you got rid of it?" he asked.

Mom nodded.

"I'm so relieved," he said. He took a long sip of tea.

"But that time D—" She cut herself off and pressed her lips together.

"What's that?" he asked, setting his cup down and looking at Mom.

She gave him an awkward half smile. "Nothing," she said shaking her head. "I'm curious about it though. I mean sometimes I could use a little, you know…" She wrung her hands. "Especially when—" She cut herself off again, this time her body and face was frozen.

"Especially when what?" Older Uncle asked in a taut voice.

Mom wrapped her arms around herself. "Nothing," she said again. "It's nothing. When I told Dae-sung about those Indians he smiled. 'Can you blame them?' he asked, 'Those poor bastards just wanted to get near the hottest girl in the club.' But I insisted that I didn't like them or trust them. Dae-sung got all serious. 'You better get over it,' he said, 'because they just contributed enough money to TSP to put Rocky through university one hundred times.'" She exhaled a slow breath. She sipped her tea. "But I can't get them out of my head. They were so awful. I could've easily just—" She didn't finish. All she did was clasp her hands over her head.

"Thankfully you didn't," Older Uncle said.

Mom dropped her hands to fidget with her ring. She swallowed hard.

Older Uncle pressed his temple. "Those men, they don't sound like regulars or anyone I've ever seen. And I wasn't there for that deal." His forehead puckered. "Can you describe them in more detail?" he asked.

"Not really," Mom said with a shrug. But then her eyes narrowed. "They were dark and sweaty and smelled gross. Like curry and wet dog. I was scared."

Older Uncle tapped his chin.

Mom bit her lower lip, then tried to smile before she said, "I'm sure Dae-sung took care of it. I'm sure they'll never bother me again."

Older Uncle didn't say anything. He was peering out the sliding glass door. A few minutes later he whispered, "Please let me know if that ever happens again."

This time Mom didn't say anything. But I saw her slide her hand into her pocket...

"Black coolie freak," Strike mumbles.

I track Ha-na. I'm a wolf after all. She's a little lost lamb.

No one's paying attention to the black coolie. She skulks along the edge of the wall until she falls into the back of the long line of students at the buffet table. Her wavy hair oozes down her back, like the black sludge in the bathroom sink drain if our house cleaners miss a week, and coats her cheeks.

The kid in front of her is digging around in his backpack. He pulls out a folder. As he slings his backpack onto his shoulder, he ends up dropping the folder. Loose papers spill out, fanning near his feet. Before he even moves, Ha-na's already crouched. Quick as a wink she gathers up the papers and stacks them neatly on the folder. She looks up at the kid from her squat, smiles, and then holds out the thin pile. The kid glares at her as he snatches his papers and folder. He whisks back around without saying one word of thanks. Ha-na drops her head. A soft but frustrated exhale escapes from her slightly parted lips.

Strike rolls his shoulders. Cracks his neck. "What do you think, boss? You want Patch and me to handle it?" he asks.

I nod. They know to keep it mostly to words. Maybe a little shoving. But never beyond that for a girl, even a girl as nasty as Ha-na.

Patch and Strike exchange half smiles.

"Shall we?" Strike asks him.

Patch nods, then springs up.

The two of them take their time swaggering towards her.

Ha-na's arms are by her side, but she starts waving a hand to Pavarotti's bold voice.

I rip the stylus off the record. *She's not allowed to enjoy my music.* When I look back, her hand has stopped. *That's better.*

She inches forward in the slow line. Then she cups her mouth and nose and sneezes. Not once. Three in a row. Three high-pitched kitten sneezes.

My mom sneezed the exact same way. I thought my mom's were so adorable. But from Ha-na...

I fast tap my shoe. My fists ball up under the table. *Relax.* I light up another cig to take the edge off. Three quick draws in a row before exhaling three large smoke rings.

Braid taps my shoulder. "Watch this, boss," he says holding up his cell phone. "Let's give Black Coolie a little appetizer."

I smile inside. My boys and I have Ha-na's number. We made her give it to us awhile back when we were into prank calling. And she knows she better answer our calls, or else. She knows she better not change her number, or else.

Braid speed dials on speaker, keeping his eyes on her.

She pats a pocket on her uniform skirt. She reaches in, pulls out her cell, and checks. She frowns, then shoves the phone back in her pocket without answering!

Before I have a chance to get worked up, Patch and Strike reach her. They sandwich her. Patch lightly pushes her.

Her head and shoulders don't droop like usual. She actually stares at Patch.

Strike brings his mouth to her ear. "Ugly. Fat. Black. Coolie," he says in a loud voice. Then he presses one hand on his chest, the other onto his mouth and fake retches.

A hush falls over the entire dining hall. All eyes are on the three of them.

Ha-na still doesn't make like she's going to retreat, she even glowers.

That's when I make my move. I saunter over, hands in my pockets, chin slightly lifted. The only sound—my shoes striking the hardwood floor.

Strike swats at her hair. Patch goes to push her again.

"Stop," I boom.

My boys drop their arms and step back.

I plant my feet in front of her, an uninterested look on my face. I flick my cigarette stub on the floor. Smash it with my sole. I look at her. "Pick it up," I order.

She doesn't move.

I take out my gold pocket watch. "You have thirty seconds."

Some sharp inhales around the room, then silence. It's so quiet I can hear the *tick tick* of my watch. I count the ticks in my mind. Thirty. Slide my watch into my pocket. "Pick it up. Now," I say, reaching for her shoulder.

She crams her hand into her pocket and pulls out a folding knife. She fumbles with it.

I retract my hand. I cross my arms and watch her, intrigued.

Finally she gets the blade to swing out. She goes into an awkward attack stance, one I'm sure she saw in some knife fight scene in an action film. Her hand trembles when she thrusts the knife in my direction. "Make me!" she yells, her angry expression and voice kind of cute like her sneeze.

I raise an eyebrow. I almost forgot what I asked her to do because I'm so amused. I laugh hard. Double over at the waist like a prawn. The last time I laughed was…let's see…that's right…never.

My boys bust out laughing too. Soon everyone in the dining hall is whooping.

The roars and shrieks immobilize Ha-na. She's stuck in a back stance, brandishing her dainty little knife.

Cute sneeze. Cute expression. Cute voice. Cute knife.

Cute is for Mom.

My laughter stops as my jaw clenches. I glare at Ha-na with my deadpan face and push back the right side of my uniform jacket.

Her eyes widen.

In one graceful pull, I produce my knife. Its blade glistens when I carve the air in front of her. I toss it up and catch it. "You were saying?" I growl.

Ha-na presses her lips together into a resigned line. She closes her blade, looks away as she slides her baby knife back into her pocket. Then she bends down and picks up the cigarette butt.

"Eat it," I say running my finger over the sharp edge of my blade.

She crinkles her nose and twists her lips. She looks at me one more time before she shuts her eyes and tilts her head back. She lets the cig butt dangle over her open mouth.

All eyes are on her.

She lets it drop.

"Chew," I say.

She does. Slow. She gags. Her eyes fly open. She frowns and chews faster. Tears pool in her eyes, but she blinks them away.

"Swallow," I say.

She does. She stands still for a second before grimacing and shuddering.

I smile inside. *Not cute anymore.*

6.

"Mommy, Mommy! Look! Look!"

A child's bubbly voice comes at me on my left. My head drifts in that direction, and there at the end of the bench is a little boy, maybe five or six. He's kneeling and bouncing up and down like he's on a pogo stick.

He points to my hand. "A dragon! A dragon!" he squeals.

My arm is stretched out on the backrest. I'm gripping the top. I grip tighter to make the colors of my beast pop. I roll up my sleeve, watching the boy.

His eyelids stretch far apart when he catches a glimpse of the dragon's body on my forearm. He looks at me, then back at the tat, pushing his tongue out of the side of his mouth. Slowly he brings his trembling finger towards the dragon's fire.

When he's a centimeter away, I quick jerk my hand up to meet his finger.

He shrieks in giddy terror, pulling his hand back fast. He cradles his finger. His eyebrows bump together as he inspects it. When he realizes he didn't get burned by the fiery dragon, he looks at me and smiles.

I smile inside. I want to tousle his hair the way my dad used to tousle mine when I'd trace his tats.

That's when the kid's mom grabs his hand. Her face goes from pale to pure white, like new chalk. "We have to go now," she whispers, avoiding my eyes. "It's getting late."

I count the black buttons on her thin overcoat. Three.

"I don't want to go," the little boy whines. "The dragon wants to play!" He tries to wrestle his hand away from her.

She tightens her hold. "We're going. Right now!" She yanks his hand and drags him away.

He looks over his shoulder and waves.

I make my dragon wave back.

When mother and son are out of sight, I turn back to the Han.

I'm still. The way I want to be—need to be—after a walk.

Deep breath of cool air. Slow exhale.

Then a breeze. It skips over the surface of the gray water, coaxing gentle waves. Tall buildings in the distance pose as sleepy giants while the setting sun fights bedtime like a three-year-old, throwing its brilliant arms all over in protest.

I'm about to get a cig when my cell vibrates. It's Braid.

"Where, boss?" he asks.

"The alley."

"Ok."

I light up and inhale. I wait for the smoke to nuzzle my lungs. Right on time it gets comfy inside, all warm and secure. The way I bet that little boy gets when he cuddles with his mother. When he's not playing with some young thug.

I knock on the bench three times before I get up and head to Yeongdeungpo. The sidewalks are ultra crowded, but I still arrive at the meeting spot before my boys.

The alley is as straight and narrow as one of the pipettes we use in chemistry class, buildings packed tight, roofs jutting over the ground enough that it's way darker in there than on the well-lit street where I am.

I enter, cobblestones underfoot and gloom all around. There are two soft lights hanging further ahead. My foot ends up kicking an empty can. It ricochets.

When my vision adjusts, I see a pair of eyes glowing yellow from behind some trash cans. They move toward me. It turns out to be a thin and scraggly alley cat. It reaches me and trills as it rubs up against my shoes. I go to pet it but my fingers stop short. I quickly pull my hand away. It's probably filthy. Germy. Wish I had some scraps of food for it though. Then a low growl from the back of the alley. Suddenly a large tom is swiping his paw at my little friend. Another growl. Another swipe. A hiss and next thing I know, both cats are gone. I stand alone in the shadow.

It's quiet except for the occasional squawks of the old timers haggling for Chinese imports on the main strip.

A gnawing ache in my gut. Then it rumbles. I press my belly, imagining the mother and son from earlier sitting down together for dinner. What did she make tonight?

A light wind flits and with it the pungent fragrance of wok charred garlic and ginger. *Mom's dakgalbi.* I think about the last time she made it for me.

She was wearing her yellow apron. Yellow, her favorite color. The scent and sputtering sound lured Dad and me to the kitchen. We peeked in and exchanged glances. He smiled at me, then rubbed his tummy and licked his lips. Mom looked up to find us loitering near the door. She fake scowled, then chased us away with her wooden spoon.

The magenta letters of Zero Cafe gleam under a small bulb. An unexpected gust rattles the splintered wooden door open a crack. Another whiff. This time of sesame oil.

I check my pocket watch. 5:55 p.m. Five minutes until my boys show up.

I toe walk from cobblestone to cobblestone, skipping exactly three in between. There's an old wooden pole under a dim streetlamp. Eight meters away I'd say. On top of the layers and layers of stapled advertisements for upcoming events, a white paper with a big red "X" in the middle—an ad for a well-known beer—calls out for my blade's attention.

Thunk.

The tip pierces the exact middle of the X.

Heavy footsteps. One set is distinctive. Braid's. He always misses the heel strike on the third step. I turn around. Sure enough.

"Boss," he says, stepping into the low light. Patch and Strike are right behind. They're all slick as usual in our mini TSP matching suits. Their white band collars almost sparkle.

We stroll into the restaurant. Only a few tables are occupied, the diners chatting in hushed voices.

We don't wait for the host. We don't have to. We seat ourselves at our private table because our perks aren't just in school.

A server rushes over carrying a large tray of banchan. He arranges the small plates of side dishes around the grill that's in the center of the table. He reaches into his apron pocket and pulls out an ashtray. He sets it down.

Smoking is banned in public places for most people. But we're not most people.

He prepares the charcoal.

We order soju and marinated beef short rib. The server recommends the spicy pork belly.

"Everything tastes better extra spicy, with a little extra gochujang," Mom said. She ruffled my hair. "Right, Rocky?"

"Extra spicy," I say to the server.

The server flashes a smile, then hustles away.

Our first bottle of soju arrives quick. Braid holds the bottle off to the side and gives it a good swirl. The liquid tornado inside mesmerizes me. He supports his right arm with his left hand and fills my shot glass. Then he fills Patch's, Strike's, and his own.

"Gunbae," I say, holding up my glass.

They raise theirs but take care to keep them a tad lower than mine. "Gunbae," they echo.

We drop our heads back and shoot.

Braid pours another round. He meets my eyes but then quickly averts his. "Did you hear what happened to Kang Dong-geun?" he asks.

I scowl inside. *No! How many times do I have to remind them that my dad doesn't tell me shit?* I keep my face blank when I shake my head.

"Your dad killed him," Braid says.

It must be true. My second-in-command always gets the fresh intel from In-su, his roommate/older cousin who just happens to be one of my dad's right-hand men, the ones who wear the red pocket squares.

I sip my soju and try to play it cool. "That Southern Gate Pa asshole of a boss must've deserved it," I say.

Braid doesn't say anything.

I spin the ashtray. Count the seconds until it stops.

Braid's eyes dart back and forth. Patch and Strike stare at the table.

"What?" I ask.

Braid takes a sip. "Your dad—"

I massage my temples. "What already?"

Braid clears his throat. He blots the thin layer of sweat on his forehead with his handkerchief. Finally he opens his mouth. "Your dad, he didn't just kill him." He pauses to look at me. "He tortured the guy."

Duh. Tell me something I don't know. "Yeah, well, he must've deserved it," I say all nonchalant.

My boys trade anxious looks.

I light up a cigarette and take an extra long drag, then release three smoke rings. I drape my arm over the back of my chair, holding the cigarette loosely between my index and middle fingers. "What did he do? Piss on the guy's face, then bury him alive?"

Braid's quiet as he refills our shot glasses.

That's when the server arrives with another bottle and our meat. He lays the short ribs on one side of the mesh grill. There's a sizzle followed by the sweet and smoky aroma of caramelizing sugar. Then he puts the spicy pork belly on the other side. Another sizzle, this time followed by a complex spicy and gingery smell.

"Anything else?" the server asks.

I shake my head.

The server leaves.

I glance at Braid as he flips the short ribs with the tongs. His eyebrows are almost touching.

"Rocky," he says, "you need to know what your dad did."

I take a draw on my cig and exhale my frustration in a smoky mess that ends up drifting into Braid's face.

He doesn't fan it away. He keeps his eyes on me.

I'm bored, but I go along with it. "Yes? What did he do?" I help myself to a piece of meat and take a bite. It's delicious. Tender.

"Got all the scoops from In-su. He, Chul-moo, and Do-hyun had to hang the guy upside down, you know, so all the blood would drain into the guy's head and he'd stay conscious as long as possible." Braid pauses. Drums his fingers on the table. His face turns sallow. He grabs his water and chugs it. Then he looks over both shoulders and lowers his head. "Ok, here goes," he says. The rest comes out fast and steady, like the perfect rhythm of punches to a speed bag. "Your dad insisted on finishing up the job himself. He tore out the guy's tongue. Pliers. Gouged out the dude's eyeballs. Chisel. He used a rusty saw—" Braid gags. He quickly cups his mouth and manages to keep the contents of his stomach in his stomach.

I stop chewing. I want to spit it out, but I wash it down with the rest of the soju in my glass.

Patch is frozen. His good eye huge. His chopsticks extended out in mid-air.

Strike drops his chopsticks. They land with a plink on his ceramic dish.

Braid's sweating like he's just sprinted five kilometers.

None of us say a word.

I push my plate away. The soju won't touch me now. Might as well have been drinking water.

Strike goes for his soju but then changes his mind. Patch scoots his chair back. Braid hangs his head.

The server comes back to us like that and our meat and banchan untouched. He starts wringing his hands. His face and voice drop when he asks, "Is everything alright?"

I wave him away because I'm not about to spend any extra time reassuring him when my own mind is freaking out…

There's no way my dad could do that! Could he? No. No way! It's supposed to be an eye for an eye. But what if he really did it? Is he a psycho? Gangsters aren't supposed to be psycho. Gangsters are supposed to be methodical. Professional.

But my face will never give me away. I'm calm on the outside when I look at my boys and say, "Let's go."

They nod. We get up, file out of the restaurant, then plod up the alley, crammed shoulder-to-shoulder between the walls.

Loud scraping sounds.

I look up. Fours thugs—wannabe thugs is more like it—dressed in white tank tops, gold chains (fake, I'm sure), and jeans approach, dragging bats. Even in the faint light I can tell they're not much older than us. The one on the far left smacks his bat on the wall.

Soon we're toe-to-toe. I cross my arms and stand in a slight lean back. I stare at the jerk in front of me.

He gives me a half smile. "You rich boys are on our turf," he says. He brushes the lapel of my expensive suit. "You're gonna have to pay the toll."

I give a slow stroke to my sideburn before I slide my hands into my pockets and widen my stance a little. Then I bring my hands together in front of me and steeple my fingers when I say, "I guess you haven't heard."

He scoffs. "What's that?" he asks all cocky.

"That we've always owned these streets. So, unfortunately, it's you and your boys who need to pay the toll," I say, my voice smooth as my mom's homemade chilled tofu.

"Good one," he says with a chuckle. He elbows one of his cronies,

"Listen to this guy," he says. He and his poser boys all laugh. But when he realizes we haven't backed down a bit, he shuts up and straightens his face.

His boys follow his lead and zip it.

They exchange confused glances, then charge at us, bats swinging.

I roll my eyes, already in a defensive stance.

The ensuing scuffle lasts less than five minutes. We disarm the punks easily because they're all bark and no bite.

Braid has one of them in a headlock. Patch has his knee in the back of another who's facedown on the ground. Strike's side kick sends a third flying a few meters back. That unlucky bastard ends up slamming into the brick wall.

I'm standing over the leader with his own bat angled dangerously above his skull. Fear flashes in his eyes. Under any other circumstance, I would've come down hard—but not into his skull because I'm not a murderer—I would've smashed the bat into his arm, or maybe his gut.

He tore out the guy's tongue. Pliers. Gouged out the dude's eyeballs. Chisel. He used a rusty saw—

I dry heave.

The guy gives me a baffled look.

We're not murderers.

I drop the bat, clutching my stomach.

He reaches for it.

I kick it out of the way. "Let's split!" I call to my boys, then start running towards the brightly lit street.

My boys are right behind.

7.

The sounds of Seoul far below fade as Pavarotti belts out *Caruso* for me. He declares his love for a girl as he looks into her eyes...

And I close my eyes, slide down a little on the loveseat. I tilt my head back and let my limbs fall loose. Time stops the way it can only stop out here on the balcony—only in the presence of my number one tenor's sorrowful exuberance. The Onkyo won't give a shit about hours as long as I'm here to lay down the vinyl. The weather pays no attention to the city's minute-to-minute schedule, enjoying instead the moment in untethered spontaneity. But each second for me is stuck in sweet rewind. When everything was good. When everything made sense.

I sniff. Is that sizzling scallions?

Mom with a close-mouthed smile, flipping haemul pajeon. My mouth starts to water. I tug at her yellow apron. She looks at me and winks. She slowly reaches down, her hand on my cheek, soft. Then Mom, Dad, and I are together on the balcony. Mom and Dad are on the loveseat. I climb onto Mom's lap, curl up, releasing waves of calm like a kitten purring, paws tucked, napping in a patch of sunlight. The three of us watch the rain.

We are together.

We are together.

I smile inside, my eyes still closed. I try to melt into the cushions.

It feels nice. So nice. Like when it's cold outside but my hands are wrapped around a ceramic cup filled with hot tea. *I sip and swirl the liquid. It soothes my wintry soul, coaxing it out of hibernation into the warmth and promise of spring...*

Click clack of Dad's house slippers. One-one, two. Two-one, two. Louder. Three-one, two.

Time rushes back and slams me into the present.

We are not together.

My eyelids fly apart. A strong wind is punishing rush-hour traffic on the expressway below, and rain is coming down hard. The beeps and hum of gridlock stab me. Pavarotti's heartbreaking voice becomes a crowbar, ripping my heart out. I push down on my chest with both hands.

Dad slithers through the open sliding glass door. He sits on the far end of the loveseat and stares at his wet, gray kingdom.

Dad lifts his small bowl of makgeolli without taking his eyes off the cityscape. I pour, keeping my head down but my eyes on him. He takes a sip, then sets the bowl on the table. He brings out a chrome cigarette tin, one I've never seen.

What happened to the one that matches Mom's? Matches mine?

His finger goes back and forth over the cigs. They're not Dunhills!

Why not?

Finally they land on one and he plucks it out. MARLBORO.

Dad lights it, takes a drag, and exhales twin smoke rings. "Got a surprise for you," he says.

That's the last thing I expected him to say. I feel a tingling all over because the last surprise Dad got me was my knife, and it just happens to be my most prized possession. "Really?" I ask, my voice flat though inside I'm a twittering canary.

He nods.

He takes another draw and releases three rings this time. "Don't you want to know what it is?" He doesn't look at me.

"What is it, Dad?"

He turns his head to me and smiles. "A brand spanking new Genesis coupe. It's parked downstairs. Tsukuba red. I know you like red."

My jaw drops. I'm speechless.

This is how he shows me he cares.

Exactly ten seconds later, I get a grip and bow my head. "Thank you, Dad. I'm grateful," I say. And I really am. How could I not be? I mean, it's not even my birthday. Or any special occasion. It's a just-because gift. A sleek sports car just-because gift.

"It's got massive horsepower. Eight hundred. Drove it home myself."

"I can't wait to drive it," I say. I light up a Dunhill and take slow draws delighting in the buzz. I exhale clouds of smoke. I'm floating away with these clouds...

But then a sinking feeling. *What have I ever done to deserve something so expensive?*

"Let's take it for a spin later. What do you say?" Dad asks, his eyebrows raised.

"Sure, Dad," I say, my voice strangled now because I'm submerged in an ocean of guilt.

He half smiles and looks back at the view.

I stare at the cigarette between his fingers. "How's business?" I ask.

"Fine."

Must be. A new Genesis coupe—and I'm certain he's souped it up—is like, what? Forty-nine million won? At least.

Suddenly it hits me.

With Kang Dong-geun out of the way, is Dad making even more money now? Is that why he splurged on a new car for me?

I stub my cig, then scratch my head. "Anything new?"

"No."

I look at him, but I can't find any evidence of lingering regret over a recent murder in his expression—every facial muscle is relaxed, his skin is smooth and taut, his eyebrows are straight, and his lips are slightly curved up at the ends.

The rain decides to take a break. Dad turns back to the delicate mist hanging over the city. But I'm stuck with an image of Kang Dong-geun's mutilated body dangling upside down in some vacant building. Blood draining, a slow drip, drip, drip...like the last bits of rain on the balcony's top rail.

I grab my bowl and down the rest of the makgeolli. I need a smoke. I reach into my jacket for my Dunhill tin.

Dad and the weather are calm, but I'm not. Not anymore.

My hands tremble. I fumble with the lid. When I finally pry the tin open, I drop the cig I pick and three more roll out.

Great, four.

I feel around on the chilly tiles until I find them. I put three back and slip one between my lips. I whisk the lighter off the table, but it takes me a few flicks to get the flame to catch. I light up and inhale. I try to hold it in for a few seconds but end up coughing out a pathetic mess of smoke.

And what's on my mind.

"What did you do to Kang Dong-geun?" I spit.

I hold my breath as my completely unboss-like delivery prods Dad's low-key vibe.

He squints at me, his jaw tight. "Nothing," he says in an almost playful voice. He wags his finger. "Come on now, Rocky, you know you're not supposed to ask me about work."

"But I heard—" I start.

He shows me his palm. "Stop," he orders. Two lines appear between his brows. He cracks his knuckles, then his neck. "We're not talking about that." He takes his last sip of makgeolli.

No sense arguing. My arm cogwheels out with the bottle, and I refill his bowl.

He returns the favor. I count the seconds it takes him to refill mine. Four. *Uh-oh.*

He takes a drag and exhales a thick stream. He waves the hand holding his cigarette. "You just focus on your studies," he says. "Keep up those top marks."

I fight back. "Dad, why can't I help you now? I don't need school to be a good boss. I—"

He cuts me off. "I've told you how many times now?" He rolls his eyes. "No boss talk, no TSP talk—until I say so." He pauses. "All you need to do right now is study." He chuckles. "You're the smartest person I know. Who else can memorize *The Netter Collection* before the age of twelve? What other students don't have to go to cram school and still be number one?" His expression hardens again. "You'd certainly be a great surgeon like your mother wanted," he mutters.

This is the only time he brings up Mom—when he avoids discussing the gang with me. And I hate how he refers to her. Always "your mother" or "she." Never "my wife," or "my dear," or "Bo-young." Always in a matter-of-fact or angry voice. Never tender, never loving.

Annoyance churns in my gut, bubbles into hot fury, and I erupt. "Don't you miss her? I mean, she was more than my career counselor!"

Dad doesn't say a word.

"Did you even love her?" I snap.

Nothing.

I cross my arms and sit back, shaking my head. "You know what? It doesn't matter. Maybe I'll just quit school now. I'm the only Yi descendent. I will take over—"

"No!" he bellows. "You will keep going with your education until I say you're done!"

Now the veins in his neck are throbbing.

This time I can't *not* argue. I use a different tactic. My next words barrage him like machine gun fire. "Older Uncle is dead. You banished Younger Uncle. There's no one else."

Dad's face goes from pale to fiery red in six seconds, as fast as I know my new Genesis coupe can go from zero to one hundred kilometers per hour. His knuckles are white from how tight he's squeezing his fists. He gets up in slow motion. Without warning, he smacks the makgeolli bottle. It flies off the table and smashes into the far wall, then drops to the floor. It doesn't shatter. I watch the pearly alcohol trickle out. I'm itching to count the seconds until it's empty, but Dad's hovering over me like a raging bull. His heavy, hot breath scalds my face. He goes to say something, but groans instead. He raises his fist, his chest heaving.

Panic propels my blood in scared, stiff spurts through my body. I don't dare move, and I'm not sure if I'm breathing. Somehow I keep my eyes dead center on his.

I count how long we stay like this.

One, two, three, four.

Four. Again.

Shit.

He raises his fist and punches the wall above my head. "Ungrateful little shit," he growls. He glares at me for another second, then storms back inside.

I turn around to look at the wall. Four small splotches of blood.

8.

I linger in the classroom doorway, quietly beating the outer wall. *Four dropped cigarettes. Four second makgeolli pour. Four second staredown. Four blood splotches…*

Around and around it goes, the four fours of yesterday. Death squared is holding me hostage, and there's no escape in sight. My eyes dart around the classroom, searching for a sign, something that offers liberation.

There's nothing!

I start to sweat. But then—the wall clock. Bingo. I focus on the second hand. If I enter when it gets right to twelve, I'll escape misfortune. It doesn't matter how I know this, I just know this. And I can't mess it up.

A bit earlier or later and…

I'm not going there.

Second hand at nine.

My hands in my pockets.

At eleven.

I lift my chin.

Twelve.

I swagger in, exhaling relief.

A strong formaldehyde smell shoves itself up my nose. I get a little dizzy, but I don't let it show.

We're dissecting frogs today. That means I get to use a knife, or rather a tiny scalpel, to cut once living flesh for an entire hour and a half.

Everyone else is already at their lab tables, gawking at the pale, slimy frogs supine on their stainless steel dissection trays, as if they're napping.

I scan the room for an open table. There's only one at the front. Next to Ha-na.

Ugh.

I look to the right. Should I strong-arm the wimpy boy out of his table? Straight ahead of me. Charm one of the popular girls? They'd give it up easily to me. The table, that is.

Well, that too.

Not that I've ever had sex. Or a girlfriend. But only my boys know that.

The teacher calls the class to order.

Too late.

The table next to Black Coolie it is. I stroll over, making sure not to step on the grout lines.

I slide on the latex gloves.

Ha-na's eyes are glued to her frog. Her gloves lay in wait on the table. Her hands are under the long sleeves of her uniform jacket. She's scratching her arms. Her hair's out of her face. Tied in a high messy bun.

I don't think I've ever seen her entire face without a bunch of frizzy hair in the way. She looks different with her naked face.

My cheeks get warm.

She's actually kind of pretty.

Her dark skin is flawless. Gleaming obsidian eyes. Sharp, good nose. Full lips tinted strawberry tangerine.

I wonder how they taste…

My eyes move down her physique, following the curves of her full bust, small waist, and broad hips. She's curvy S-line perfection.

If that's fat…

I imagine erotic stone sculptures of full-figured Indian women. I can't help it. I can't help that I've flipped through my dad's book on the ancient Khajuraho temples once or twice. Or fifty times. And why wouldn't I? I mean the Indian temple complex is a UNESCO World Heritage Site and I like architecture and history and…artwork that's liberal. Sexual in nature even. Trust me, I didn't need the descriptions under the photos.

A celebration of the female form. A celebration of female power.

I guess I don't hate everything Indian.

The room spins. I reel.

High on lustful thoughts or the formaldehyde? I don't know, but I need to settle down.

I grip the edge of the table and stare at the dead frog. That sobers me up. Fast. And I'm glad my boys aren't here to witness this...I don't know what the fuck this is.

Ok, Ha-na's beautiful, it's true. But still a weirdo black coolie.

I clench my jaw and tap my scalpel three times on the tray.

Beauty is not to be trusted.

Beauty lets you down.

Beauty leaves you.

I realize I'm not thinking about Ha-na anymore.

The teacher rambles on about frog anatomy.

Mom waltzes onto the balcony. The train of her elegant gold chiffon and lace gown glides over the cool tile the way her hand glides over Dad's cheek a second later. She must be a real angel. That's what Dad says two seconds later. He captures her hands, but he can't trap her eyes— they're on me. Mom smiles, but her eyes are a little wet, a little sad.

Mom's sprawled out, naked, on her bed. Fast asleep at noon. Snoring soft. Her eyeliner and mascara have leaked black all over her face. There are big knots in her messy hair. I wonder if she's cold. I grab her bathrobe and drape it over her body. That's when I notice several yellowish-brown marks on her upper arm.

My heart is throbbing...

I'm squeezing the scalpel so tight my hand is shaking. Pins and needles prickle. I open my hand and the scalpel falls, clink, onto the tray.

Ha-na peeks over. Our eyes meet. Hers are sad and shiny, like puppy dog eyes.

Don't. Trust. Those. Eyes.

I look away. To the teacher.

"Alright, class. Get to work," he says. He points to the chalkboard. "When you're ready to identify all of these organs, call me over."

I take a deep breath, release it slow, and get to work. I spread the frog's limbs. Pin them to the dissection tray. Forceps. Gather the skin near the hind legs. Lift. Small cut. I move my forceps up the frog's body to keep the skin separated from the muscle. Continue the incision, taking care to only slice through the skin. Then perpendicular cuts between the front legs and hind legs. Fold the flaps back. Pin them down.

My steady hands and zoomed-in eyes perform their tasks with great skill even though this is my first real dissection. The worms in the park don't count. I used to "operate" on them when I was a kid. I picture myself as a surgeon in a tense operating room. Scrubs and surgical mask. Bright lights. Everything blue, white, and sterile. My faithful residents and nurses assisting me. The reassuring beep of the machines monitoring my patient's status.

I frown inside. Shake my head. *I'm not going to be a surgeon. I'm going to be the TSP boss.*

My body tenses and my hands tremble, but it doesn't affect my performance. With precision I pick up the frog's muscle near the hind legs and repeat the process of cutting, peeling, and pinning down that layer. Then I remove the fat bodies shrouding the organs. That's when I see the eggs.

All of a sudden it's hard to breathe, like that time Patch sat on my chest when we were play-fighting as kids. My hands quiver like they're having their own mini-seizures.

My eyes wander. Most of the other kids are struggling to cut the skin or muscle. But not Ha-na. She's done. She pinches her forceps together, then uses the end to push aside some organs for a better view underneath.

Is she looking for the spleen? Wait a minute. You can't let this loser beat you!

The teacher's heavy footsteps. They fade. When I look up, he's left the room.

I glimpse back at Ha-na. I smile inside. A sly smile. "Hey, Black Coolie," I call.

She stops her work. She remains still, forceps in hand, like an unsure rival surgeon. She doesn't even blink. Her lips are slightly parted.

"My cigarette wasn't enough? You hungry again?" I ask.

She doesn't answer my questions.

The popular girls giggle. I look over my shoulder at them. I catch their eyes and point to Ha-na with my chin.

Two of them, Mi-sun and A-ra, saunter over to Ha-na's table.

Mi-sun stands in front and leans on her elbows. She glares at Ha-na.

A-ra stands next to Ha-na. "Answer him," she orders.

Ha-na doesn't.

Mi-sun and A-ra exchange glances.

A-ra scoffs. "This beast doesn't know her place," she mutters. She looks at me.

I consider making Ha-na eat an organ, but formaldehyde is toxic. I'm not trying to kill her, just make her life hell. Another tactic. I pretend to scoop out some frog organs and smear them in my hair. Then I say, "I think she needs a hair treatment, don't you?"

A-ra flashes me a devilish half smile and nods. She tugs at Ha-na's bun with her gloved hand.

Ha-na's hair plunges down her back.

Then A-ra sticks her hand in Ha-na's frog and digs up a handful. She rubs the squishy organs between her gloves.

Everyone in the class is chanting. "Coolie, Coolie…"

A-ra takes her time to give a good show. She slowly lifts her hands above Ha-na's head. As she lowers them down, the chanting gets louder.

I'm almost expecting Ha-na to whip out her knife, or do something to defend herself. But she doesn't.

A-ra's organ-filled hands settle on Ha-na's head. She drags them down, leaving a lumpy film on the length of Black Coolie's hair.

Then I make the mistake of looking at Ha-na's eyes—she's crying.

A-ra and Mi-sun are laughing. So is the rest of the class. But I'm not. My face is stony. My eyes are stuck on Ha-na.

She removes her gloves. Then she moves quickly to the door, keeping her head down. A second later, she's gone.

Ten seconds later the teacher returns, and everyone stops laughing. He must have just missed Ha-na because all he says is, "Who's ready to identify the organs? Raise your hands."

9.

Strike elbows Patch. "Check out that hottie," he says pointing to three o'clock.

Patch presses his forehead on the large window-wall for a look. He turns to Strike, his eye bulging, his jaw dropped, and carves an hourglass in the air.

Strike starts to smile but then draws his face back when Patch raises his eyebrow up and down. "Hands off, big boy," Strike says, "I saw her first."

Patch shrugs, then hangs his head in mock disappointment.

Strike looks at me. "Hey, boss, think your dad would get that pissed if I snuck down there for a quick digits mission?"

All I do is stare at him.

Braid's mouth hangs open, a little gasp escapes. Patch swallows his lips and shakes his head.

None of us say anything because what do you say when your boy is volunteering, not for a "quick digits mission," but for a suicide mission? One thing's certain, you don't say, *yeah, go for it*! with high fives all around.

See us being anywhere "down there" would set off an unfortunate chain reaction—TSP security would spot Strike immediately, report his presence to their big boss, and Dad would most certainly get "that pissed."

And then Strike might end up like Kang Dong-geun.

"Down there" isn't just anywhere, it's the main room of my dad's club—Club Orion. "Down there" is a huge space with a dance floor, DJ booth, sitting areas, and two full service bars. "Down there" is what everyone else in Seoul knows as the hottest nightclub in the city. But "down there" is a front. What most people don't know is what's in the back—secret rooms for TSP business.

My boys and I aren't allowed anywhere "down there." Not in the front. Not in the back. Dad's rule. He only lets us chill here in the VIP room that's tucked away in an upstairs corner.

Incidentally, my boys and I call it the VIP room, my dad calls it our "clubhouse."

I scoff inside.

So babyish.

But then I sly smile.

Dad has no idea that I've spied on one of his secret "down there" back room meetings. It wasn't easy. It took the cover of darkness and some serious ledge parkour to get to a small outer window. Never brought my boys, never would. It's way too risky for them. I mean, my dad might pull a Kang Dong-geun on them, but not on his own son.

Strike rubs a hand over his itty bitty stubble. "So guys, what do you think?" he asks with a shrug, "Is it a go?"

We still don't answer him.

Strike's eyes land on me, and I drag my index finger horizontally across my throat.

Strike gives a nervous chuckle. "Never mind. I'm a dumbass." He knocks his skull, hard. "There," he says."Just knocked some sense into myself." He looks at his crotch and wags his finger at it. "No, gochu. It's not happening," he loud whispers to it.

Patch breaks into silent hysterics.

Braid smiles. "Yeah. You and both your heads better stay up here."

Strike sulks, mumbles a couple of unintelligible words, and goes straight back to ogling the girl.

"Good old horny Strike," Braid says as he fills my glass with more soju.

"Any new intel?" I ask him as I light up a Dunhill and take a couple of draws.

He shakes his head. "Nothing, boss."

I release a curtain of smoke from one side of my mouth. "What about that new street stall? The one near Hongdae station?"

Braid nods. "Oh yeah. That. Sorry. Shouldn't be a problem, boss. Scrawny guy selling cell phone cases. Single. No kids. Raking in the dough. Especially busy from four to seven."

"Good," I say. "We'll hit him up tomorrow. Seven-thirty." Long drag. Three smoke rings.

"Ok," Braid says. A satisfied smile stretches across his face. He lights a cig, then sits back to enjoy his smoke.

I look at Strike and Patch.

Strike makes some joke about sex.

Patch lunges at him, puts him in a headlock, and goes on a noogie rampage.

It's business as usual up here, but, speaking of sex, it's not just me that's never had it. Neither have my boys. And it isn't for lack of opportunity. First of all, there's the popular girls at school. I know for a fact that they'd get with us in a heartbeat. Or we could go to one of the red-light districts that "don't exist" according to some official city reports. Or I could ask my dad. It's not like he hasn't tried to hook my boys and me up before.

I don't know about my boys, but I have a specific reason why I'm not rushing to do the deed. It goes back to something my mom told me.

It was late afternoon. The sun was finally shining after monstrous clouds had been covering it for a week. I crept quiet as a mouse into my parent's bedroom. Dust particles floated in the sunbeams that licked Mom's face as she lay in bed. Her eyes were closed, but she knew I was there.

"Rocky," she said, "come here."

She looked so messy, her hair, her face—like she hadn't slept in days, even though she was still in bed. What was she doing?

"Please, Rocky, come here. I'm so tired…"

I was afraid, but I made myself go to her.

She stroked my head. "Oh, Rocky," she said, her voice sad.

I studied her face. There were big bluish-black bags under her eyes. Her lips were cracked, whitish…

"My handsome boy," she said.

There were reddish bumps on her tongue like tiny pebbles when she spoke. Red scratch lines on her cheeks and neck.

She patted my head and smiled.

"One day you're going to have a girlfriend, maybe someday a wife," she said. "Be kind. Don't hurt her..." She paused, touched her neck. "Listen to her. If she tells you she doesn't like something, don't do it. If she's sad, help her. Don't give her bad things like—" She didn't finish that sentence. Instead, she laid her hand on a small plastic bag near her shoulder and slid it under her pillow before I could see what it was.

"Get to know her so you can trust her and she can trust you," she whispered. "So you can trust each other."

I was only six. I didn't understand her, I guess, though I did get the part about not hurting my future girlfriend or wife.

These days I don't consider myself to be the nicest person. I mean I hurt people on the regular.

My shoulders slump as I let out a quiet breath.

So it just might be possible that if I have sex, I could hurt the girl. Her feelings, that is. I'm not a rapist. That's why I made a vow to myself, to Mom, to wait until I'm in love before I have sex. Because when you love someone, you care about them enough not to hurt them.

Right?

I haven't been in love yet, so I haven't had sex yet. I sit tall, nodding inside, because it makes perfect sense to me.

Braid gets up and strolls to the window, hands clasped behind his back. "So who's this hottie?" he asks with a chin up.

Strike jabs his finger into the window.

Braid's eyes widen. "Damn," is all he says. He bites his knuckle.

The three of them drool over three o'clock. Hungry wolves stalking a juicy lamb.

I yawn and meditate on the Korean hip hop instead. The bass reverberates through my chest, my new heart beat. A loud boom boom.

Out of the blue, Braid slams his palms into the window and yells, "Shit!"

I jump a little.

"Six o'clock!" he shouts, then mashes his forehead against the glass. "Boss," he says, waving me over without looking back. "Check out this chronic. He's tweaking…"

I get up and walk over, slow, for a look. Directly below us there's a guy writhing on the ground, scratching his skin like every centimeter of his body is covered in mosquito bites. I cringe inside. At the rate he's going he'll draw blood for sure. "So he is," I say, then take an unhurried drag. I hold the cig against my chest. I'd never admit it to my boys, but I've never seen a tweaker before.

"How the hell did he get into the club?" Braid mumbles.

Strike tsk tsks. "Such a waste of a countryman," he says, then pauses. He turns to me with his arms crossed. "Boss, how about only selling to the Japanese when you're in charge. Let them suffer the way they made us suffer all those years." He holds a finger up. "Oh and also the Americans."

Patch nods.

I take my last drag and let my head fall back to exhale. Slow smoke puffs float like fluffy clouds in the dim room. "Money is money," I say, crushing the stub in the ashtray. "Japanese. Americans. Koreans. White. Black. Brown. Yellow. As long as they pay, we'll sell to them." I once heard Dad say that to Older Uncle.

Braid punches the thumb side of his fist into his mouth. "Fuck," he whispers. "That guy's hating life even more right about now."

I look. Two thick TSP dudes in black suits drag the tweaker's ass literally across the crowded dance floor. The sea of sweaty, drunk bodies parts to let them pass.

I give a slow stroke to my sideburn. Wonder where the druggie got his stuff. TSP? If so, he'd have gotten the purest meth in Seoul. *Too much will kill you.* Something else I heard straight from the horse's mouth.

My hand settles on my knife handle, surreptitious trace of my stars, my name.

The security haul the tweaker to the bar, kicking and squirming. Suddenly he's still. One of TSP guys lets go to readjust his grip. The tweaker curls up quick like a millipede and starts picking. Slow at first. Then fast. Faster.

A dull prodding sensation deep in my gut turns into a stab.

My boys remain fixated on all the excitement.

The tweaker is picking, picking, picking…

I clench my jaw. It's as if I'm so close to remembering something, but that something stays just out of reach.

I squeeze my eyelids. Strain. *Come on, come on. What is it?*

It's right there. It's...

Damn.

My eyes rip open because my brain hands the something to me on a platter. But not a platter piled high with delectable treats. An enormous mound of shit.

I poke my head into the bedroom, careful to keep the rest of me hidden.

Mom's crouched in the corner, her stringy hair sticking to her sweaty face. Her red eyes are huge. She's picking the skin of her bare legs and arms. "Spiders!" Mom whispers.

My little body tenses.

"Get off me," she growls.

She rubs the back of her hand down one side of her face. Black streak. Maroon smudge.

"So many spiders," she mumbles.

Is she in pain? Maybe she needs my help. I force myself to take a few steps into the room, though my heart's ramming into my chest.

She's picking. Picking, picking, picking. "Spiders all over..."

I look. I don't see any. "Mom?" I ask, in a faint, hesitant voice, "Are you ok?"

She stops picking for a second and lifts her head. Our eyes meet, but she's looking through me.

"Mom?" I ask again, this time my voice quivering. It's then I notice what's strewn around her. An empty bottle of soju tipped over like a fallen bowling pin. A worn-out baggie of funny looking crystals. Something that looks like a tiny fish bowl attached to a glass straw. A lighter.

I guess she drank the soju, but what's all the other stuff for? I want to ask her, but she drops her head and frantic pick, pick, picks.

Everything gets blurry. Then my eyes rain…

Far off voice. "Boss?" Tap on my shoulder.

I turn my head.

Braid's looking at me with huge eyes and a puckered forehead. "Boss, you ok?" he asks.

I nod. Doesn't feel like me nodding.

"You don't look so good," he says.

"I'm ok."

"I don't know. Your face. It's so pasty." He looks at Patch. "Get the boss some water," he says.

Patch nods.

I look past Braid, at the tweaker. *It can't be true. No. No. No!* I tap my foot like there's no tomorrow.

Braid stares at my moving foot.

I lift my foot and stomp to make it stop.

"Boss…" Braid says, reaching for my shoulder.

I pull back, but then the room starts to spin. I wobble, hold my arms out…

"You better sit down, boss," Braid says grabbing my arm.

He eases me onto the sofa. I don't feel better. My body is freezing outside even though there's a fire raging inside.

Patch hands me a bottle of water. I chug it. It doesn't thaw my exterior. It doesn't put out the inner fire.

Braid sticks his hand in his pocket. "You're dripping," he says.

I touch my forehead, the back of my neck. I'm drenched all right.

He pulls out his handkerchief and hands it to me.

I flip it over and over. Then I try to strangle it, but it doesn't have a neck.

"Your forehead, boss," he says.

I wipe it. "Thanks."

There's an unopened bottle of soju on the table. I give it the evil eye. *Alcohol. Drugs. It all makes me sick.* My hands tingle from how hard I'm making fists. Then, without warning, I jump up and grab the bottle, fling it across the room. It shatters when it hits the concrete wall. Soju sprays and dribbles.

I don't count the shards, I can't because all I see is red. "No more drinking!" I shout.

Pinging of two voices and nods of agreement.

Sure thing, boss.

Ok, boss. No more drinking.

One silent nod.

Five eyes are on me.

Tears pool in mine. I look away, shut, and squeeze. Can't cry in front of my boys. I swore I'd never do that again. And I haven't. In fact, I haven't cried in front of anyone in ten years. Ever since that day in the school stairwell, one month after my mother left and two months after my father drifted further and further away into TSP.

Tears poured. I buried my face in my hands. My body shook as I cried quietly.

I don't know how long I stayed like that.

When I lifted my head, three of my classmates were squatting in front of me. They didn't say anything at first. I brushed my face with my palm and put on a blank expression. They introduced themselves. Jung Chul-soo. Kwan Han-bin. Cho Joon-ho.

(Two years later: Braid, Strike, and Patch.)

Patch used to speak back then. He put his chunky hand on my shoulder. "We're going to the swings. Come with us."

I looked at Braid and Strike. They nodded.

I stood up and held my hand out to Braid, the way I'd seen my dad hold out his hand to people after a business meeting. Braid slowly lifted his hand to meet mine. He shook it. Electric. Shook hands with Strike and Patch. The same. *Handshakes like jumper cables to jump-start me.*

I open my eyes. My boys are huddled around me. Just like that day ten years ago. Patch puts his hand on my shoulder. He smiles a gentle smile. It says more to me than any amount of words.

I stand up, at attention. Turn to Braid. He bows. I extend my hand. He gives it a firm and resolute shake. *High voltage.*

"No drinking," Braid says, bowing again.

I nod.

Strike and Patch bow. I hold out my hand to each of them in turn.
We shake. *High voltage, times two.*

Handshakes like jumper cables to jump-start me.

Some things never change.

10.

This Hongdae alley is alive after dark—flashing neon restaurant signs, bright street lamps, hungry people swarming like bees in a brick-walled hive, buzzing with gossip and honeyed small talk.

Dad taps my shoulder.

"Yeah?"

"That's where we're going," he says, pointing to a vertical yellow sign that has **GRANDMA AHN'S BIBIMBAP** written in red characters.

It's the last restaurant before the ivy-covered dead end.

"The best dolsot bibimbap in Seoul," he says. "Your older uncle's favorite."

I don't respond because I'm busy counting the delicate leaves on the creeping tendrils.

Dad doesn't notice. He slaps my back and laughs before he says, "Can you believe this place is my age? That's old!"

I turn to look at him. "You're not that old," I say, all serious.

He pats my back. "Very kind of you, young man."

I like when Dad's this way—not angry. It happens sometimes.

We walk a little more and reach the tiny restaurant. I squat in front of a three-shelf display case near the entrance. My mouth waters at all the plastic replicas of meals. The dolsot nakji bibimbap on the bottom shelf catches my eye. "What was Older Uncle's favorite?" I ask.

"Traditional, of course," Dad says.

I lick my lips at top, center. Then I stand and follow Dad into the restaurant. I smell gimchi and sesame oil. I can almost taste the warm rice. The gochujang. The blend of meat and vegetables.

It's crowded and noisy inside, but of course we've got our own private table in the back corner waiting for us. Perks.

The server brings water and asks what we'd like to order. He fast-taps his pad with the eraser end of his pencil as he waits.

I count the taps. *Don't be nervous, server. The big boss is in a good mood today.*

Dad orders the traditional and a beer.

I'm on twenty when the server turns to me.

I decide the dolsot nakji bibimbap will have to wait until next time since we're here for Older Uncle's birthday. "Traditional," I say. "And water."

The server scurries away.

Dad looks at me with a wistful expression. "Your older uncle and I used to eat here all the time. He was—"

His cell rings. He checks the screen and scowls. Shrugs, then says, "I gotta get this."

I nod.

"Yes?" he answers with an irritated tone. He listens. "Gimpo?" He pushes his chair back and shoots up, catching my eye. He points to the front and mouths, "I'll be right back."

I nod again.

He hustles outside, grunting disapproval.

Our drinks arrive. My dad's beer glass is tall and frosty. I imagine taking a drink. *Crisp. Refreshing.*

But I follow my rule. *No beer. No alcohol at all.* I gulp some water. *Not the same, but it'll have to do.*

I take another sip, wondering what's going on in Gimpo. Dad's got a TSP warehouse there so it must be gang business. He and Older Uncle purchased the Gimpo warehouse when I turned six. Dad took me there once. When he told Mom where we were going, she objected, like she always did about me and gang stuff.

"There's no way I want you taking Rocky to a gang hangout, of all places." She frowned. "Why not a playground? Or the zoo?"

Dad winked at me. Then he turned to Mom and started in on some magic. He embraced her. Whispered something in her ear. Kissed her cheek. Another whisper. Neck kiss.

She pushed him away. "You're such a charmer," she said, still frowning but less.

I got to go after all.

Dad let me sit in the front seat of the black Genesis sedan he had then. I thought it was the coolest thing ever. Such a classic ride, and I was dressed so fancy.

"The suit looks good on you," he said.

I puffed my chest out a little and smoothed my suit—the same kind my dad was wearing. Then I looked out the window, grinning inside.

As Dad drove us further away from Seoul, more and more trees sprung up from the earth. I peeked at him. He looked over at the same time and reached out to tousle my hair.

We arrived at a huge empty warehouse with broken windows and rusty doors. Older Uncle greeted us. I tugged on his suit. He crouched down in front of me. I cupped his ear and whispered, "Where's Younger Uncle?"

Older Uncle shot my dad an uneasy glance.

My mom had the same anxious look whenever Younger Uncle was mentioned. A week before, my parents got in a big fight over his name. My dad's face was crimson when he screamed, "Who does he think he is? Some hotshot that can come into my home and take what's mine?" He was glaring at Mom. "No one takes what's mine. People take what I give them!"

I stayed hidden under the end table. Watching. Listening. All I could think was *Younger Uncle's not a thief...*

Dad reached into his pocket and pulled out his handkerchief that was tied in a small bundle. Held it up. "I know you want this, huh? Anything to forget him, right? Well, here, take it," he said throwing it to Mom.

She caught it and tucked it into her pocket. She looked away.

Then Dad yelled, "Good riddance to him forever!" He punched a hole in the drywall before he stormed off.

I pressed my hands over my ears. But I kept my eyes on Mom. Her shoulders were hunched, her lips clamped shut. Tears slid down her cheeks.

Older Uncle put his hands on my shoulders. "Well, Rocky..." he started, but my dad grabbed my hand. I looked up at him, my lips parted still. His expression scared me so I didn't say a word.

"Let's go," Dad said.

The three of us marched into the warehouse. There were a bunch of young men already there, all dressed in the same classy black suits.

My fingers skimmed my band collar.

"Thirty new recruits," Dad said.

He squeezed my hand as we walked. The men parted and formed two even lines. I wriggled my hand out of Dad's and ran to the end of one line. Then I proceeded down the row with my head tilted back, inspecting each man's eyes. When I got to the end of the row, I did the same for the opposite line.

The last man had muscles bursting out of his suit. He also had a glass eye. I stopped in front of him. I lifted my finger, I had to touch his hard eye. But then he drew back one side of his jacket. He motioned with his good eye to the top half of the gun that jutted out of his waistband.

I didn't flinch, but I felt a patch of warm wetness in my pants. I hoped the man didn't notice.

"Rocky!" Dad called.

I ran to him.

Dad held one of my little arms up and Older Uncle held the other. "Long live Three Star Pa!" they declared.

In the chorus of booming cheers that followed, I forgot I'd peed on myself. I let go of Older Uncle's hand and tucked my thumb in my belt. I smiled inside.

But right now I'm frowning because those days of Dad including me in TSP business are long gone, and I don't know exactly why.

No more time for frustrated regret because Dad's back. He sits and scoots his chair forward. "The beer," he says in delight. He takes a sip. "Ahh…"

Our food arrives, as does the extra gochujang and gimchi that I requested. The server sets our culinary works of art in front of us. I rub my palms together and smack my lips. My eyes feast on the edible rainbow. Green: cucumber, zucchini, spinach, crispy gim, and soy bean sprouts. Brown: mushrooms and thinly sliced beef. White: radish and rice. Yellow and white of a fried egg. Light brown sesame seeds sprinkled on top. I add the translucent yellow sesame oil. Then I heap on the rust red gochujang and more gimchi. "The most important things," I say.

He leans in and whispers, "Just like your mother." Then he grins, it's a genuine grin.

I stare at him for a second, but then my growling stomach redirects me. I brandish my stainless steel spoon as if it's my knife and plunge it into the stone pot, mix everything, three stirs at a time. The egg yolk oozes, coating all the other ingredients. That part never gets old. When

Mom made bibimbap, she'd give me two fried eggs arranged in my bowl like two eyes.

"Make them cry," she'd say, encouraging me to break the yolks.

One more look at the colorful swirl of rice, vegetables, and beef. Then I shovel an enormous bite into my mouth. I chew it slow. *So delicious.* No wonder it was Older Uncle's favorite. Maybe it's my favorite now too.

I raise my glass. "To Older Uncle," I say. I look up and thump my chest over where my stars will be someday. A proper salute for a proper boss.

"Rocky..." Dad says, his voice and face suddenly stern.

"What?"

He shakes his head. "No gang stuff for you yet."

I consider arguing but end up just crossing my fingers under the table because, *um, yes, gang stuff for me now, thank you very much.*

Dad raises his glass. I take care to keep mine a little lower.

"To my older brother. Happy birthday. Rest in peace," he says.

We clink glasses. Dad looks around. "Oh...he loved this place," he says. He takes a small bite, then lays his spoon down. He interlaces his fingers on the table and looks at me. "This one time, he ate two and a half stone pots. He had a big appetite. And a big heart." He pauses. "Too big. Too kind sometimes," he mumbles before going for another bite.

"He used to bring me boxes of Pepero when you were working late. All different flavors. This one night he handed me a bag of all chocolate and said 'Sorry, Rocky, I bought you ten but I ate five. Tell you what, I'll read you three stories tonight to make up for my gluttony.'"

Dad laughs. He scrapes some of the crusty rice from the bottom and brings the crunchy goodness to his lips but stops short. He face becomes ashen. He sets his spoon in the pot. "I told him to slow down," he says. His eyes are shiny. He opens his mouth to say something else, but nothing comes out except a long, slow breath. He closes his mouth and tries to smile.

Older Uncle died a month after the Pepero evening. "A massive heart attack," is what the doctor told us when we got to the hospital.

It was a nightmare seeing Older Uncle in the state-of-the-art intensive care room. My larger than life Older Uncle looked so small in the bed. So fragile with all those machines and tubes. There was even one shoved in his mouth. His eyes were closed. He didn't move or talk. When something beeped, I'd jump.

He died a half hour later. *One continuous beeping sound.* The scariest sound I've ever heard.

And though my heart didn't stop working like his, it broke a little.

I miss him so much.

But at least I knew what happened to him. I saw it with my own eyes.

Mom on the other hand, she completely disappeared one day. Poof. Gone. Just like that, I didn't ever see her again. I didn't see what happened.

Then again, even when she was around sometimes I didn't see what was happening. Like that day she ran inside their bedroom, crying, a desperate look on her face...

She slammed the door behind her. It almost hit my forehead because I was at her heels. I turned the knob. She'd locked it. I tested the knob again. It was still locked.

I pressed my ear to the door. She was bawling. I knocked hard and called her name.

Dad was gone, but Older Uncle was there.

He laid his hands on my shoulders, knelt down, his soft eyes peering into mine. "Come on, Rocky," he said. "Let's go. Mommy needs to rest."

I didn't budge. "But it's not bedtime," I protested showing him my watch.

Older Uncle half smiled. "I know, but sometimes grown-ups need to..."

"Need to what?"

He looked away and fiddled with his medallion.

"Need to what?"

He shook his head. "It's nothing."

"But—" I began.

He stood up. "Tell you what," he said. "Why don't I read you a story?" He raised his eyebrows and held up a finger. "No! I've got a better idea. Let me tell you a wonderful tale." He waved his hand with the tiger tat. "It's about a tiger family deep in the jungle..."

My eyes followed the tiger tat I wished I had on my hand. But then I turned back to the door, back to my mom.

Older Uncle didn't give up. "Do you think you have enough guts to hear it, Rocky?"

I looked over my shoulder at him, he was petting his tiger hand.

"Yes. Let's go," I said all boss-like. I marched to the living room. He was right behind me.

We sat side by side on the sofa. He cleared his throat and began. "There once was a tiger family…" I kept my eyes on his tiger tat and listened.

Many, many words later he tapped my shoulder. "Do you know what happened to the Mommy tiger next?"

I shook my head.

"She started eating more and more ginseng root. At first it made her strong. And the pain in her claws was gone. She felt invincible. She could finally growl back at the mean Daddy tiger. She could stand in front of their cub and protect him…"

A loud scrape. I blink. Dad shovels crispy rice into his mouth.

Older Uncle had the best stories. I wonder if Younger Uncle used to tell me stories. I try to dig up some Younger Uncle recollections. Nothing, so I do some math. He was gone before I was six. Four? Five? Urgent questions about Younger Uncle stockpile in my head like grenades at a military base, and before I can stop myself I pick up a grenade, pull the pin, and toss. "Dad?" I ask.

"Yes?"

"Did Younger Uncle come here with you and Older Uncle before you banished him?"

My body stiffens as I brace for an epic Dad detonation.

Dad stays chill. He takes a slow bite. Sips. "Sure," he says. "All the time." He smirks. "Good times." Then he chugs the rest of his beer, slams the glass when he's done. He pushes his unfinished pot away and his chair back. "We're done," he says. He gets up and heads for the door.

I want to stay and gobble up the rest of my bibimbap. But I know better. I risk one more big bite, then rocket up and follow him.

Our server is clearing a table near the front. He looks up as we approach. His eyes get huge. "Excuse me," he says, edging closer to my dad. He bows, then asks, "Was everything ok?"

I'm expecting my dad to pretty much ignore the server. Maybe a simple nod or wave of the hand.

But no.

My dad shoves the server.

The poor beanpole of a guy goes flying back into a wide support column.

Next thing I know, Dad's in the server's face. "The food was cold! Unacceptable!" he screams. "If that ever happens again…" My dad lets his voice trail off as he drags his finger across the server's neck. Then he raises his fist and makes like he's going to punch the guy in the face.

I push in between them, but my dad's already lowered his fist. He looks back and forth between the server's scared-shitless face and my confused one. A second later he starts cracking up. "The food was fine. I'm just messing with you," he says.

The bug-eyed server manages to spurt a nervous chuckle.

Dad slaps the guy's arm, a little too hard if you ask me, and then turns away. "Come on, Rocky," he says. He heads to the exit.

I follow but look over my shoulder at the server. We exchange quick glances. *I'm sorry, I know how you feel.*

11.

I walk. Time evaporates like rain on hot summer asphalt. My polished shoes do what's necessary—step over each crack.

The cracks get closer.

And closer.

Above, a beautiful yellow chrysanthemum arrangement lines the top of a huge gate.

Yellow.

Mom's favorite color.

Yellow chrysanthemums, whatever may come.

My eyes feast on the brilliant lemon flowers. The gate's charcoal gray-tiled roof slopes up at the corners. Clouds seem to shoot out of it, smearing the rich blue sky with almost vertical lines.

I look over my shoulder at the bustling city behind me. Then I turn around and breath in the ancient splendor of Namsangol Hanok Village. With my next step, shoulders slumped, hands in my pockets, I time travel to the Joseon era.

The courtyard commands a taller, prouder walk. I oblige.

Everything is softer. The pressed dirt path. The yellow green leaves on the persimmon trees. The red and green pavilion, a baby dragon sleeping next to a slow stream.

I walk the winding path. There are traditional houses on both sides. All the doors are open, inviting me in.

But I can't stop. I can't take a break. Things won't be right.

I keep walking.

Large brown earthen pots lined up in…quick calculation…three rows of nine. Twenty-seven.

A light breeze nudges the little purple spring blossoms. They sway shyly on the tree branches that dangle over the onggi. Petals flit, littering the lids, the ground. A delicate, fragrant mess.

A heavier breeze follows. It pushes me, but my steps remain steady.

The cracks spread out again, pushing me out of the peaceful village. I slouch into modernity. I walk. Crowds. Chatter. Beeps. Brakes.

Pass by a bunch of backpacked kids. *Nine.*

They're huddled together like a school of fish swimming home after Saturday school. They're yapping away and giggling. Hopping on and off the sidewalk.

I slink by them. Weave between all the people. I'm in a bubble. Nothing can touch me.

I keep walking.

Minutes. Hours. I don't know. I stop only when the Han spreads before me. Vast. Magnificent. Calm. Like an untouched refuge.

Home.

I ignore the people. The picnickers. The bikers. The strollers. They're in some other parallel universe.

This is my world.

Deep breath.

I'm safe. I'm home.

But alone.

I spot an empty bench near the water's edge. I sit, indulge in a smoke. I hold my cig at arm's length and inspect the perfect thin barrel. I take a long drag, then try to exhale my doubts and fears. I tap the white rod three times, watching the ash sprinkle and float.

My cig and I enjoy the Han. The ripples are hypnotic. I lose count.

I crush my cigarette stub, then flick it.

I look around on my left and do a double take because there aren't many guys with fully shaved heads and red pocket squares roaming around Seoul, let alone hanging out at the Han. But here's one standing partially hidden behind a tourist couple.

Chul-moo? What's he doing—

Before I finish deducing, a child wails on my right.

A little girl, cheeks slick with tears, is pointing at the river. "My ball! My ball!" she screams in between sobs. Her parents are running down the path. They catch up to her.

"What happened?" her father asks.

"Are you ok?" the mother wants to know.

The little girl rubs a sleeve across her nose. "The river took my ball!" She starts bawling again, really loud.

Her parents sink down to her eye level.

"It's ok, we'll get you a new one," her father reassures, stroking her head.

"But that's the one Su-bin gave me," she blubbers.

The little girl suddenly stops crying. Her jaw drops, and her eyes get big. Then she smiles.

I look where she's looking, and my heart stops for a second.

It's Ha-na.

What's she doing here?

My hand drifts toward my knife but stops when I see what it is that she's doing—lying prone on the sidewalk, stretching her arm over the water. Seven seconds later she gets up, holding a bright pink rubber ball. She digs in her pocket and pulls out a handkerchief. She carefully dries the ball, then walks toward the little girl.

The girl runs toward Ha-na.

They meet in the middle.

Ha-na squats down and gives the girl the ball and a close-mouthed smile.

The girl hugs the ball. "Thank you," she says with a slight bow. She looks at Ha-na and grins so big I can see that her two front teeth are missing.

The parents catch up again.

Ha-na stands, bows.

"Thank you," the father says.

"So kind of you," the mother says.

"No problem. You're welcome," Ha-na says with another bow.

The girl pats her ball, whispering something to it. Then she looks at Ha-na and flashes another grateful smile.

Ha-na watches the family walk away. The little girl turns around and holds her ball up to kiss it. She waves at Ha-na.

Ha-na waves back. After the family disappears, she hugs herself. She turns around and goes to her gleaming white blanket that's spread out on the grassy area. Her things are neatly laid out to hold down the corners—a sketchbook and pencils, a water bottle, a lunch box, and a thick book. She sits cross-legged and picks up the book. She takes one last look at the river before burying her head in its pages.

My skin prickles. I rub the sleeves of my suit to make it stop, but it doesn't. I try picking. Once, twice, three times. To no avail. I pick faster. There's no crystal in my body, but I'm picking...

Suddenly the itchy tingling is gone. I drop my hands.

But then my mind starts picking at itself...

How could I ever?

12.

"Line up!" Braid shouts.

There's a plink plink of water somewhere in the abandoned building.

"What are you waiting for?" he growls.

The five junior boys fall into place, hunched over like guilty convicts brought before a judge, knowing that they are about to receive the harshest sentence. Resigned to the fact that it very well could be the death penalty.

I smile inside. *I have no intention of killing you morons, but I'm not about to give that away. Guess what, imbeciles? Time to sweat it out…*

Patch and Strike flank the line while I lean against one of the cracked support columns off to the side and smoke.

Braid paces all furious in front of the juniors like he's amping up for battle. "You had a week!" he cries. He stops and faces them. "And none of you delivered? It was only two hundred thousand won each!" He lets out a loud, frustrated breath and drops his head. Shakes it. "This is bad. So, so bad," he whispers.

And you are good. So, so good, at this, Braid. Just like how my dad says

In-su is so good at his TSP duties. I take a long draw on my cig, let the smoke seep into my lungs. *The apple doesn't fall far from tree.* Braid's parents died when he was five, so his tree has been In-su ever since.

Braid jerks his head up and yells at the top of his lungs, "Which one of you will take the beating for the rest?"

Furtive glances. Nervous shifting. A trembling hand goes up.

"You? Pock Face?" Braid yells. He scoffs, then glares at the shaky junior. "Are you ready to die for these losers?" he asks, drawing a line over the other four.

Pock Face doesn't open his mouth, he only wobbles like he has no bones.

"Stand here," Braid orders pointing next to himself.

Pock Face hesitates.

"Now!" Braid hollars.

Poke Face minces his way forward.

Braid nods at Patch.

Patch lumbers over, stops when he's face-to-face with the kid. Cracks his knuckles, then his neck.

Pock Face swallows at the bull of a senior before him.

Patch has this wrathful look in his eye. I've seen it many times before. It's a toned-down version of the look he had the day he stopped speaking. The day he couldn't save his little sister from the stray Southern Gate Pa bullet.

I look away for a second. Take a hard drag. By the time I release the smoke from my mouth and lungs, Patch has already taken off the jacket of his school uniform. Slowly, he rolls up the sleeves of his dress shirt. As soon as he makes the last fold, his hands ball up. He scowls and smashes Pock Face's chest with a one-two punch that sends the boy flying back.

Pock Face and the two juniors directly behind him end up in a pile on the dusty concrete foundation. Pock Face presses his chest, gasping for air.

Braid marches over to them. "Who said you could sit?" he roars.

The three of them look at each other.

The scrawniest dares to whisper, "No one."

"Who said you could talk?" Braid screams.

They all look down, lips set in matching grim lines.

"Get up!" Braid orders.

They do.

"Line!"

They arrange themselves on either side of the other two.

Then Braid nods at Strike.

Strike saunters over. He stops in front of the first one and starts doing small, but fast, downward bounce steps while throwing air punches.

I chuckle inside because I know that he has no intention of punching these bastards. They have no idea what my man Strike is about to deliver.

And deliver he does. Warmed up, Strike goes down the line and gives a different, perfect kick in the gut to each junior. Side. Roundhouse. Back. Hook. Spin.

Their trashy asses end up scattered like garbage in a landfill.

Strike smooths his uniform, then meanders between the junior junk, spitting on each of their faces along the way.

Of all four of us, Strike's the most sophisticated with his fighting techniques. That's because he's a taekwondo grandmaster who's earned his ninth dan belt already. He once told me that he didn't set out to excel in the martial art, it just turned out that way because his wealthy parents were away on extended vacations most of the time. So he basically grew up in a nearby dojang.

I suck on my cig. Let the smoke twist out of the side of my mouth.

Braid crouches near them. "You losers are lucky today," he says. "We'll give you an extension until tomorrow. But have the money to us before school starts or else you will die." He makes like he's going to punch Pock Face. They all throw their hands up and do a collective flinch. Braid whips Pock Face with his braid before he gets up. Then he starts laughing his ass off.

I smile inside because we've succeeded in breaking these wimps. We don't have to beat the complete shit out of them today because I know they'll come through with the money tomorrow. I take a pull on my cig and a quick inhale of the dead air. Blow out three identical smoke rings, just like my dad. I glare at the juniors. They're lucky I'm not my dad. Because if on the off chance they don't pay up, we won't kill them like he probably would. We'll just make their life so miserable they'll wish they were resting in peace. I flick my cig and crush it with my shoe.

The junior boys are still on the ground, contorted and wheezing.

"Tomorrow," Braid yells. "Or else!" He moves in front of Pock Face. He swings his leg back. Holds it there for a second.

Pock Face inhales sharply and immediately curls up into a tight ball.

Braid snickers before he lets his leg sweep forward in a powerful kick to Pock Face's compact body, like it's a soccer ball. Then he turns to me like nothing. "Ready?" he asks as he flings his braid over his shoulder.

I nod.

My boys and I exit the building without another look at our victims. We step into the bright day, all victorious. I let my head fall back, stretching my arms to the side and a little behind like they're the edges of my superhero cape. The sun rays congratulate me with warm cheek kisses.

Then, hands in our pockets, a spring in our step, we peacock side by side, relishing the thrill of a job well-done. We take a couple of shortcuts through some whimsical alleys until we end up on a busy sidewalk. We approach an American fast food restaurant, Burger House.

Strike pats his belly. "Greasy burgers and fries," he says in a dreamy voice. "Anyone else hungry?"

Patch presses on his belly and nods.

"I could use some fuel," Braid says, "But let's make it quick. I wanna get an hour or two at a noraebang before I have to meet In-su."

"Sounds good," Strike says. He pokes Braid in the arm. "But this time, don't be a mic hog." He shakes his head and says, "Bad form, my friend, bad form."

Braid smiles. "Yeah. Ok." He looks at me. "How about you, boss? Will you sing today?"

"Maybe," I say.

Strike frowns. "Maybe means no," he grumbles.

I nonchalant shrug.

We go into the burger joint and order. Four double cheeseburgers, four fries, and four vanilla milkshakes. Our food is served up fast. We carry our trays to an empty table. Sit.

Strike devours his food before the rest of us are half way through. He sits back, needles a toothpick between his bottom right molars, and looks at Braid. "You said quick, didn't you, slow poke?"

Braid stops chewing long enough to smirk but doesn't bother to respond. Instead, he finishes the bite, then sucks down half the milkshake. He pushes his tray in so he can rest his elbows on the table. He looks over both shoulders before he stoops and whispers, "I gotta tell you guys about Woo-jin."

Fuck. Wish I knew this stuff first!

"What's that?" I ask, squeezing my knife handle. "That he's a prick?"

Woo-jin is Kang Dong-geun's son. He runs a mini Southern Gate Pa gang at his high school. I'm willing to bet he's hoping to take over SGP someday.

Maybe we have something in common—big dreams to be big bosses.

But with Kang Dong-geun dead, Woo-jin's succession isn't a sure thing. I'm guessing it's only a matter of time before my dad drives Southern Gate Pa out of the city. Then Three Star Pa will be the most powerful gang in all of Seoul. And someday soon I will be the big boss of the most powerful gang in all of Seoul.

Woo-jin will be nothing.

I wonder if Woo-jin knows about all that. I wonder if his dad used to tell him things about their gang. I wonder what his mom's like...

Braid nods. "Well, yes. But what I was going to say is that some girl he and his boys were bullying killed herself last week, jumped off Mapo Bridge. They found her body floating in the Han. She left a note, naming them as her tormentors. Apparently they'd been harassing her every day for over three years. Anyway, they're all in juvie now. Woo-jin..."

I stop listening because I'm lost in my head.

Ha-na.

My hand is still on my knife handle.

Braid taps my shoulder. "Boss?" he asks.

I look at him and then at Strike and Patch. They're staring at me.

"Boss?" Braid asks again. "Are you ok?"

I don't move. I don't say anything.

But my thoughts race well over any speed limit, as if they're my Tsukuba red Genesis coupe in the middle of a time attack at the Tsukuba Circuit.

I don't want anyone to die, not even Ha-na.

My foot taps silently, three times.

There are many ways I'm like my dad, many ways I want to be like my dad, but killing people isn't one of them.

I'm nauseous and antsy, a strange combination.

Suddenly I get up and walk away.

I've got to walk.

I know I'll end up at the Han. That's good because I have to check it. I have to make sure Ha-na's not in it.

My boys call out.

"Boss, where are you going?"

"What about singing?"

I don't look back. I don't respond. I walk. Out the door. Take a right. I keep going. All the way to the Han.

13.

Exactly three hundred and three steps from our penthouse doorstep, Dad and I turn left onto a cobblestone side street. Window boxes filled with flowers in every shade of pastel line the walls. The petals rustle in the midnight breeze and greet us with the gift of sweet smells.

I let my fingers bob over the rough brick wall. I look at Dad. He's cruising with a blissful expression. He could be a regular, happy guy. I pretend he is.

I dare to treasure the moment...

Speaking of treasure, the sky is a vast expanse of diamond inlaid black wood. I count the twinkling gems. Seventy-six by the time we're standing under the small wooden sign of our destination—Bar None—a popular late night hole in the wall restaurant.

We enter. Most of the tables are full of drunk, happy people toasting and gabbing. Everyone's Korean, except for two young G.I.'s at the back. Their uniforms and dog tags in this casual setting scream *we're so cool*. And of course they're louder and more obnoxious than anyone else in the place.

I roll my eyes inside.

One of the G.I.'s punches the other one's arm and shouts, "Man, I haven't been there since Jesus was a corporal!"

They cackle in hysterical laughter, nearly falling off their chairs.

I look away. I wish I didn't understand English. Bet these guys can't speak, read, or write Korean.

Dad and I weave through the tables to ours. Yup. Perks. We don't bother to check out the menus because we always get the house speciality.

An enthusiastic server jogs over to us. He hops to a stop and bows to my dad. "Good evening. Are you ready to order?"

Dad nods and says, "Spicy pork bone stew times two. One beer. One water."

The server bows again before he scoots away.

Dad clasps his hands behind his head, tilts his chair back a little, and looks at me. "How's school?" he asks.

"Good."

"University entrance exam is a half year away," he says. "You should start attending cram school."

"But—"

He holds his palms up. "I know, I know, you don't need it. But it can't hurt, right?"

"Why bother? I'll get the highest score in the school. Besides, it's boring." I yawn big to prove it.

He raises an eyebrow, lets it fall, then smiles. "I just worry sometimes. But your headmaster insists you're a 'genius.' I guess a genius doesn't need cram school, does he?" He pauses and shakes his head. "You didn't get that from me," he says. He taps his temple. "That brain of yours—definitely from your mother."

Yeah? *Smart mom + meth = ?* This is the only equation I haven't been able to solve. I wish there was a cram school for family mysteries.

I count the scratches on the table as my fingers drum the wood.

"You ok, Rocky?" Dad asks.

I look up. "Huh?"

He points to my busy fingers with his chin.

"Oh." I press my palm flat.

The server appears with our drinks. Disappears.

Dad holds up his beer, nods. I raise my water, keeping it a little lower than his and nod back.

The server reappears with our large stone bowls. He lowers them down in front of us.

The delicious fragrance lures me closer. I shut my eyes and lean in for a deep inhale. I get an unexpected aromatic facial steam, like the ones my mom paid hundreds of thousands of won for at the Willow Tree Spa. She and Dad went every Sunday afternoon. Dad still goes. It's kind of sweet I think, carrying on a tradition they both shared.

I pick up my spoon and stir the hot, luscious broth three times. Cautious slurp. The creamy, nutty, spicy flavors of perilla seed and gochujang bring a bit of comfort. Another slurp. This time I get a tasty prize—a piece of soft, fatty meat. I chew extra slow to enjoy the taste.

The stew is good. Really good.

But Mom's was better.

I pluck out some soybean sprouts and shiitake mushrooms with my chopsticks but end up dropping some on my lap.

Shit.

I pick the bits of dinner off my trousers. Pick, pick, pick. A couple of drops of sweat tumble off my forehead and mix with the mess. When I wipe my brow, I realize I'm drenched all over. I peel my shirt off my chest.

"Rocky, you sure you're ok?" Dad asks.

I blurt, "Was Mom sick?"

"Sick?" Dad cups his chin, then shakes his head. "No. She was always healthy." He sips his beer.

"Did she ever drink too much alcohol? I mean more than the stuff you drank together?"

He rubs his hand over his scant stubble. Squints his eyes a little. "Why do you ask?"

"It's just…"

"What?"

I stir my soup three times. "Well, I remembered something about Mom the other day. It wasn't good."

"What was it?"

"She looked sick. She was talking to herself about spiders. Picking her skin. There was an empty soju bottle. And—"

"And what?"

"A bag of crystal and a pipe. I think that's what it was." I look at him, my eyes wet. "She wouldn't do that, would she?"

Dad presses his fingertips together, then drops his eyes and exhales long and slow. When he finally looks up he says, "Rocky, there is something I should tell you." He lifts his chin a little. "It's time."

My heart flutters.

"Your mother was smart. And, of course, she was beautiful. But she had a dark side. She had secrets," he says with an inscrutable expression.

Dad's words hit me like Strike's tiger claw to the neck. Can't breathe for a second.

"Dark side?" I whisper. "Secrets? What kind of secrets?" *Like why she left*?

Dad opens his mouth. "She—"

A crash interrupts him.

Everyone in the restaurant freezes.

I don't want to look. I want Dad to finish telling me about Mom's dark side. About her secrets. But my head ratchets in the direction of the heavy sound.

A wooden chair lays on its back at a table where two young ladies are sitting. They're staring at each other with arched eyebrows. The annoying G.I.'s are hovering over them.

When the girls notice everyone's eyes on them, they look around, smiling and bowing as if to say *everything is ok.*

Everyone buys it, everyone goes back to their private conversations. Everyone except me and Dad. We hone in. We know trouble. And trouble we smell.

One of the girls says, "Please leave us alone" in Korean.

The taller G.I. with buzzed brown hair and a large mole on his cheek picks up the fallen chair. He slumps down in it and edges closer to one of the girls. Then he says in English, "Come on, baabby. Come to daaddie. I need me some I & I. Intoxication and…" He runs the back of his index finger down her bare arm and adds, "intercourse."

I'm not sure if the girls understand English, and I'm wishing I didn't for the second time tonight.

"Gimme some I & I, baby," Mole Boy says.

One day you're going to have a girlfriend, maybe someday a wife. Be kind. Don't hurt her. Listen to her. If she tells you she doesn't like something, don't do it. If she's sad, help her. Don't give her bad things…

My hand is wrapped around my knife handle, and I'm squeezing.

The second G.I., with a head full of curly red hair and a face full of freckles, staggers to the other chair. Sits.

The girls slide their chairs away. The G.I.s follow. Freckle Boy puts his arm around the girl next to him. She frowns and squirms in place.

That's it.

I push my chair back. In English I say, "Excuse me, sirs, these ladies are saying they don't want to be disturbed."

The G.I.s look at me with droopy eyes.

Mole Boy strokes the girl's shoulder and smirks.

I try again. "Please leave them be."

"Sh-shut up," Mole Boy slurs.

Freckle Boy chimes in. "Get outta here, little boy. Let the men play." He clasps the other girl's arm.

I grip Freckle Boy's wrist, my hand a vise. My eyes don't veer from his as I pry his fingers off. He jumps up, knocking over his chair. He comes at me and we're toe-to-toe.

Mole Boy scrambles behind me.

"I don't want to hurt either of you," I say. "Leave now, and you'll be ok."

They belly laugh. Then Freckle Boy gets serious. He glares at me. Throws a sloppy punch at my face. I block it and deliver the bottom of my right hammer fist.

"Awwwww!" he cries, cupping his bloody nose in both hands. He takes a few wobbly steps back.

Mole Boy puts me in a chokehold. I grab his arm with both hands and bend forward. Swing my right leg back around his calf, trapping it. Turn my body sharp and pull him off me. He lunges at me again, but I jab his trachea with my knuckles. His eyes bulge. He staggers back holding his neck.

I pull out my knife and drop into a fighting stance.

Freckle Boy grabs an empty beer bottle. He holds it by the neck and smashes the heel on the edge of the table. The bottom shatters leaving him with a jagged weapon. He thrusts it in my direction.

I don't flinch.

Hardcore stare down. Freckle Boy's face and neck glisten with sweat.

I'm not sweating anymore. In fact, I'm dry as a sheet of gim.

Freckle boy gives his buddy a confused look.

Mole Boy's huge eyes are glued to the gleaming, sharp blade of my knife. He shakes his head.

"Fuck this," Freckle Boy mutters. He drops the broken bottle. The two of them hustle out of the bar.

I slide my knife into the sheath. Smooth my suit. Then I run my hand over the top of my head. Not a hair is out of place.

I turn to the girls and bow. I switch back to Korean and ask, "Are you both alright?"

Nodding, they thank me.

One more bow before I head back to our table. Dad is busy working his stew. He looks up and gives me a proud smile.

Then my eyes play tricks on me—I think I see Ha-na in the corner.

I look again.

It is her!

She's at a table with a Korean woman who I guess is her mother. Her wide, dark eyes meet mine and narrow to crinkled slits. She looks away, muttering something to herself.

14.

The air smells of freshly cut grass, the wind is the sun's kiss, the birds—
the sky's carefree children. I hold my palm out to catch a cherry blossom
petal. It lands gently. I rub the soft pinkness between my fingers, then
release it back to the breeze. It floats this way and that, taking its own
sweet time. That's me today—a petal without any hurry.

I stretch, then amble towards my first class, touching every third
cherry blossom tree. If my finger hits one of the small horizontal cuts on
the rough bark, I touch my knife.

Soon I'm in a touch-touch rhythm. I look up. The scant pink flowers
flutter in a few bunches, like bridal bouquets. Vibrant green leaves have
replaced most of the bloom reminding me that there's only a few more
weeks of school until summer vacation. I smile inside.

Walk. Touch a cut. Touch my knife.

There are a few white wisps curling in the blue. I count them. *Six.*

Mom loved clouds. Of course: because they brought rain to her
precious city. She loved rain. But she really, really loved clouds. She had
a special place in her heart for them.

This one time, the three of us had just finished a nice picnic lunch at the Han. Dad was smoking and Mom was lying on her back admiring the sky. She laced her hands behind her head and said, "Clouds, nature's masterpiece." She looked at me. "Like us, Rocky. Like our family. Family is one of nature's masterpieces too." Then she pointed to three enormous clouds. "Those clouds," she said, giggling, "a cloud family." She sighed. "But it's not just that, Rocky. A plain blue sky, even if it's the most gorgeous azure or cerulean, is boring. A silvery cloud or two makes the perfect sky more like real life—imperfect."

Mom used to talk to me like I was a grown-up even when I was a kid. I didn't mind. At least she talked to me. Not like Dad, who talked to me less and less the older I got.

I reach for my Dunhill tin.

"Hey, Black Coolie!" someone shouts.

Obviously, it's not me. It's not Braid or Strike's voice. My hand veers to my knife.

There's a small crowd of students up ahead.

Soon the one voice becomes an angry mob. They form a tight circle, fists pumping high above their heads, and chant, "Blackie! Coolie! Blackie! Coolie…"

I move quickly, crane my neck.

It's Ha-na.

She slams her eyes shut and ducks her head under her left arm to wait it out. The kids close in. Hands push and pull at her. A loud tear. Everyone looks to the side.

One of the popular girls is holding Ha-na's sleeve in her hand. Her bracelets clink as she looks back and forth between the torn sleeve in her hand and Ha-na's exposed arm. Her eyes grow to the size of ancient rattan shields.

No one says a word. Then all eyes zero in on Ha-na's bare right arm—it looks like a Po Kim painting with its mix of flesh-colored keloids, dark reddish-brown scab lines, and more recent reddish-pink slashes.

I squeeze my knife handle.

The popular girl's bracelets clink again as she tosses the sleeve on the ground. She stomps on it, laughing. A cruel laugh. She points to Ha-na's arm and says, "You're such a dumb loser, you can't even figure out how to kill yourself!" She struts over to her. "Kill yourself, Coolie," she whispers. Then she says it again, this time louder.

Everyone starts laughing. Everyone starts chanting.

"Kill yourself, Coolie! Kill yourself, Coolie!" they yell.

That's when it bubbles up inside me, a new voice. It erupts. "SHUT UP!" I holler, pushing my way into the circle.

Ha-na opens her eyes and looks up. Our eyes meet. The dread I see in hers is enough to make me pull out my knife. My shiny blade gleams in the sunlight.

"Get away from her," I growl, gripping my knife near the side of my head.

No one moves.

"I said get away from her!" My eyes dart around from student to student.

They look away or drop their heads, anything to avoid my eyes, but they're still standing near her.

"What the fuck are you waiting for?"

No one budges yet. The popular girl even opens her mouth. "B-but—"

"No buts!" I yell. "LEAVE NOW!" I thrust my knife in the air.

That's when they finally start to take cautious steps away, keeping their eyes on my blade. A few seconds later they scatter like ants.

I slip my knife back into my sheath, looking at Ha-na.

She remembers her arm and tries to hide it behind her back, but it doesn't work. She ends up staring at the ground.

My gaze wanders down her naked arm, shoulder to wrist.

Is her other arm like that too?

My stunned eyes soften, but then harden again.

Who did it? Sure my boys and I have bullied her, but we've never hurt her like that. Did she do that to herself? I've heard of kids cutting themselves.

I lower my head.

If she did it to herself, why so many times? What's so bad that she had to—

Shit.

15.

Supplemental class ends. The students spill out of the door, straight into the chaos of the late afternoon hallway. But it takes my boys and me five minutes to finally get up and trudge our sorry asses out of the room. We move like slugs in the crowded corridor. I catch our reflection in a tinted window at the end of the hall—no swag in our walk, no air of bravado. We look so...so...ordinary. The opposite, in fact, of badass gangsters to be feared.

I grip my knife handle and trace its stars, but my badass knife doesn't cut back my patheticness.

My boys and I slog across the campus, sullen, trying not to fracture the brittle, icy air between us.

The day had started with them asking me about Ha-na's slashed up arm. I hadn't told them yet, but how could they not have heard when it was the only thing everyone at school was blathering about. And spinning. Anyway, I filled them in on what really went down, and then our gangster spirit turned into shameful cowardice. It was bad. We were the opposite of our usual selves. A few grumbles and groans exchanged in between classes, but no spitting contests. No horseplay. No hectoring. No witty banter. No not-so-witty banter. Actually, no conversation at all.

We arrive at the campus gate. I stop.

My boys stop beside me.

Braid looks at me. "What, boss?"

I stare straight ahead and say, "We're getting out of here." And I know just the place to go.

A quiet train ride to the outskirts of Seoul followed by a short walk to our destination: Nolda Land, an amusement park that's gifted many teens in Seoul—including my boys and me—a handful of fantastic childhood memories. Too bad for young kids these days, they won't grow up with their own set of good times here because this place has been long abandoned.

We pause at the front entrance to behold our beloved Nolda Land. I count the ways nature has taken it back, starting with the sun—the self-proclaimed king. His royal, fiery majesty shoots glorious rays at us from behind the gigantic roller coaster's metal skeleton.

Strike looks around, leans in. "Heard this place is haunted," he whispers.

Patch nods.

"You scared?" Braid asks, elbowing Strike. Then he turns to me, pointing to Strike and Patch with his thumb. "Boss, I don't know if these two can handle it." He pouts at Strike and offers his hand. "Poor little Strike needs to hold big brother's hand," he says in a baby voice.

I smile inside. *Things are better already.*

Strike slaps Braid's hand away. "Shut up," he mutters. "Don't come crying to me when you hear kids laughing and footsteps that aren't yours or ours!"

Braid scoffs as he kicks a pebble.

Strike mutters something else, but I'm not listening anymore. I'm lost in my memories.

I count the letters on the Nolda Land sign and the stars on the sides. *Seventeen*. Then for a second I'm a kid again, about to enter a fully operational park. The flashy oasis of fun beckons, an escape from the wasteland of bedtime. My parents and I waltz in, holding hands, me in the middle. The multi-colored lights of the rides tempt me. So do the ice cream and cotton candy booths. The games. The prizes. The clown that creeps all the other kids out but makes me laugh inside…

An easygoing wind whispers a delicate measure. Then a sudden gust blows the gates open, daring us to enter. We exchange nervous glances.

"Oh shit," Strike whispers to himself. His teeth chatter. "See?" he mouths to me.

Patch holds himself and hides his big body behind Strike, pretending to be frightened. Then he doubles over in silent laughter.

I enter. My boys follow. Braid bites his nails and bumps into Strike on purpose.

"Go ahead, assholes, make fun of me," Strike mumbles, "but you're on your own when…"

The thick layer of dead, dry leaves crunches as we walk. We pass a little red train.

Mom! Mom! Look at me! Choo choo!

We turn right and the space fighters appear. Last time I was here this was my personal fleet of state-of-the-art spaceships.

Dad! Watch this! Watch me destroy the evil galactic emperor! I will save you and Mom!

We turn left at the rusty merry-go-round. On either side of us are the bouncy animals now covered in twisty vines. The dragon bouncy catches my eye.

My dragon will burn you! Then I'll slice you with my magic sword! Ei-ya! I'll slice…

Ha-na slices…

Up ahead, the tagada looms. My parents never let me ride it when I was younger. And then the park was shut down so older me never got to try it out either. I've heard it's the scariest and funnest ride in one. Not just because there aren't any safety restraints to keep you secure as you spin but also because you're at the mercy of the tagada operator who controls the speed and direction of the ride. If he or she's had a bad day…

The unpredictable tagada, the perfect place to cop a squat. I hop on and sink onto my heels. My boys join me. We take a few seconds to light up some cancer sticks.

"Shoot," Braid mumbles, checking his watch. "Boss," he says, "just remembered. It's collection day. Those two junior boys are gonna show up at the underpass in an hour."

I'd forgotten, but I don't say that. I don't say anything. I take a long drag instead, squinting a little.

I blow dragon smoke from my nostrils and the sides of my sealed lips, stretching my arms so that my elbows balance on my knees. The ash on my cigarette rains down like tiny white and black blossoms.

"Boss?" Braid asks. He takes a drag, exhales a cloud. "How about it?"

"Not today," I say, my eyes on the tagada floor.

He nods.

Though I've never called off a job before, my boys don't question me. We stay like that, in silent squats, for awhile.

Strike crushes his cigarette stub on the tagada floor and stares at it. "So...Ha-na..." he begins. Then he looks at me with expectant eyes and Patch and Braid do too.

I give a slow stroke to my sideburn.

None of us have dared to utter "Black Coolie" since Ha-na's secret arm was revealed.

Secret...I recall Dad's words.

But she had a dark side. She had secrets.

Mom and Ha-na both, it turns out.

I wish I knew everything about Mom's dark side and her secrets. Maybe then I could've helped her. Maybe then she wouldn't have left. I never got the full story from Dad that night at the restaurant and I haven't really seen him since.

Ha-na.

I take one more long drag.

I have to help her.

I smash the burning end of my cig on the floor.

Well, at least not hurt her anymore.

Strike lights up another cigarette and takes a few drags. After he exhales he asks, "What's up with her arm, boss?"

I shake my head. "I don't know." I count the cracks near my feet.

Strike rests his forehead on his hand. "Bet she did it to herself," he mumbles. He takes another draw, exhales. "I wonder if she's done it to her other arm…"

"Probably," I say.

"That's fucked up."

None of us say anything else.

Braid puts out his cigarette, then lays his straight arms on his knees so that his hands hang limp.

I glance at Patch. He ashes his cig. His eye is shinier than usual.

"Listen," I say.

My boys look at me.

"We're gonna leave Ha-na alone from now on."

My boys nod.

"And if you see anyone harassing her, step in. Do whatever it takes to make them stop. Understood?"

They nod again.

"The new law is that Ha-na is protected," I say.

Then something kind of weird happens. We all let out long, barely audible breaths at the same time, like we're balloons with a slow leak, deflating as the tension that had been making us float gets released. And we're crumpling to the ground, only in relief.

16.

The sun is a spoiled cantaloupe. It pulls a gray blanket over itself and attempts to go back to sleep. The gloominess overhead is catching. I tilt my head back to bask in it. That, and to ignore the happy students wandering all around me. They're happy because it's the last day of school. But the shrouded sun and I, we have other things on our mind.

Sprinkles on my face, the sky's tears. They trickle down my cheeks like they're my own. I cross the courtyard to the stairwell and climb, counting the steps even though I already know how many there are. Then three paces on the landing. Ten more steps to the third floor. Twenty paces to the library.

When I get to the second floor landing something, rather someone, throws off my counting.

Ha-na.

She's wilted on a step, resting her chin in her cupped palms. Her face doleful.

She happens to look up, and our eyes meet. She crosses her arms over her chest and turns away.

Slouching, I fidget in place. Then I turn away, too.

Neither of us moves...until I can't help myself, and I look at her again.

Her peeved expression makes me wish I'd taken the back stairs. I pivot on my heels and step down, but I can't go further because it's like I'm stuck, sinking in quicksand. I grip the handrail to save myself, imagining my wrists tied to galloping horses that pull me out of the mire. Too bad they're dragging me in opposite directions, a mental torture rack. *Should I stay or should I go? Should I say something or not?*

I count the cracks in front of me, telling myself an even number means I should stay quiet and go.

Please be even.

Seven.

Shit.

I can't NOT follow my rule.

I slowly lower myself next to her. Scoot over as far right as possible because she's on the left.

A couple of students skip down between us. They look back. Their bewildered expressions remind me that I'm in enemy territory sitting quietly here next to my innocent foe.

I peek at Ha-na. She's tugging on one of the long sleeves of her jacket. Her hair shields her face from the likes of me.

I take a deep breath. "Ha-na," I say. "Are you ok?"

She doesn't answer, she only tucks her hair behind her ears.

Is she trying to hear me better?

"Has anyone bothered you recently?" I ask.

She stares at her feet.

I try again, more specific this time. "Has anyone called you Black Coolie recently?"

She keeps staring, except now her upper lip curls, and she looks away.

"Has anyone mentioned…" I swallow before I finish my question. "Your arm?"

Her fists ball up, and she's shaking a little. Then all at once she's facing me, her angry words boiling over. "How could you? All these years…so mean. But those girls at the restaurant, you help them. And you don't even know them. But me, I have to be beyond completely humiliated for you to do the right thing?" Tears race down her cheeks.

I'm paralyzed. I blink tears away, but one manages to escape, barrels down into my mouth—briny shame.

"I-I'm sorry…" I start but can't finish.

She pushes both of her sleeves up. Her scars scream *fuck you* like her expression. She shoves her hand in her pocket and brings out her knife. She pulls the blade out, then makes like she's slicing her arm. "Don't worry about it. You can't hurt me more than I can hurt myself."

"I didn't mean for you to—"

"What did you think I'd do?" she cries. "Are you completely stupid? Are you dead?" She closes the blade, crams the knife back in her pocket.

Sweat beads up on my forehead. "I'm sorry, Ha-na. Please forgive me!" I beg, my voice wobbly.

"No!" She shoots up and scurries down to the first floor.

17.

I cradle the whiskey bottle like it's a baby. I have to because my dad says these expensive Japanese blends are precious like babies. "How co-could I leave you, my love?" I slur-whisper. My unsteady hand lifts it to my lips. Big gulp. My sixth, I think, or is it my third? The liquid burns my throat, but the sweet sound of *Brindisi* soothes. Mom told me this drinking song is to a lover, but I don't care because it still encourages me to drown my sorrows in the amber elixir. It also makes me feel. Feel anything and everything with my entire being.

I raise the bottle high above my head and make a toast with Pavarotti. "Ok, buddy, you're right. Let's drink. To you!" Swig some more of the smoky harshness. "You, buddy, only you, understand me."

I close my eyes and surrender to his voice, but instead of tranquil bliss, my brain explodes. My body releases. Tension. Tears. Sad ones. Guilty ones. Angry ones.

I push myself off the loveseat. Sway. Guzzle. Stumble. *Thud*. Sharp pain on my face. I rub my tender forehead and strain my eyes. When I realize my face rammed into the half shut sliding glass door, I turn my body sideways and squeeze through the opening.

I stagger to my room. Swig. Sideswipe my bookshelf. A few paperbacks tumble onto the floor. I grab the edge of the third shelf and teeter. I manage to find my balance, but my eyelids droop and my head lolls. At some point I get steady, and my eyes land on the taped photo of my parents and me. I stare at Mom.

I lift a shaky finger, point it at her. "You!" I say, "You picked meth over me. You left us. You ruined everything. I don't need all the details, I just know it's all your fault," I whimper. It takes all my concentration to turn my finger back and jab it into my chest. "You left me!" I scream, jabbing a couple of more times.

Ha-na…

Swig.

Shit rolls downhill, Ha-na…

I hug the whiskey bottle and stroke it. "My little baby, I'll never leave you again," I whisper.

I rub my eyes, but things are still blurry. I totter to the nightstand and slam the whiskey bottle on it. I seize our family photo from the floating shelf, stare at it. Then I tear it in half. I tear it in half again. And again. And again. And again…until it's nothing but tiny bits, which I sprinkle everywhere like snow. I snicker when I'm done and grab the whiskey, chug. I go to put it on the nightstand but miss. *Thud.* Touch my face. *It's not my face.* I look down in slow motion. *It's the bottle's ass.* The beautiful liquor leaks all over my floor. I'm too drunk to count the seconds or even give a shit. I fling myself onto the bed. "It's all your fault, Mom!" I yell before I roll over. I almost fall off the bed. "So selfish, so selfish," I whisper, shaking my head. "Druggie child abandoner," I mutter. "You don't deserve my tears."

Suck in my snot. Rub my eyes, hard.

I jump out of bed and stomp to my armoire, wake up my knife. "Time to work," I say to it, squeezing the handle.

I lumber over to my designated throwing spot. The beam goes in and out of focus. I aim at it as best as I can, but my eyes drift to my arm. My sleeve is bunched up so that my skin, my tats, are visible.

...you can't hurt me more than I can hurt myself.

Mom. Ha-na. Mom. Ha-na...

My brow furrows. Pressure builds, it's about to destroy me.

I turn my blade on myself, dragging the tip through the skin of my inner forearm. Pain. But it isn't as bad as the anguish in my head. Bright red line, red relief drips onto the floor. *This is why you do it*, I think, picturing Ha-na with a fresh cut, a bloody knife, and a mollified smile.

18.

I pound the empty streets of Seoul like a drunk giant trying to sprint. I struggle to slow down. I want to walk, but my legs won't let me. I try to avoid the cracks, but the ground keeps shifting so that each of my lolloping steps ends up breaking my mother's back.

Suddenly I'm not alone. A throng of wounded, limping zombies trudge towards me. I race by them, bumping into a few who turn their heads slowly to me. My own fear pours out of their wide, shiny anime eyes. I shrink back from them and take a sharp left into a deserted alley. The sun blinds me for a second. I blink, then shield my face.

The air becomes thick, sludgy. I can't get enough oxygen into my lungs, and I start heaving. My heart drills my chest. I reach for my knife with my trembling hand…it's not there.

I'm running faster, panting and sweating. In the distance the sun attempts to hide behind a couple of skyscrapers, but its rosy amber beams leak out the sides.

A cool breeze, then my steps slow. Soon I'm walking, my breath calm and my heartbeat steady. I look down. My feet pass over the cracks. Knife? I check. It's there. I exhale in relief.

I'm at the Han's edge. The gentle water, a glossy mirror, licks my toe caps. I close my eyes with hopes of serenity, only to open them to a raging, muddled mess of frothy brown rapids. My heart sinks as twigs and debris rush by. The river's surge relays a message.

Come.

The far bank gets farther away. Out of nowhere, a long, narrow dock appears at my feet.

Come.

I step. The boards creak and tilt. I steady myself. One slip and the dark churning water would surely swallow me.

I make it to the end.

Look, it says.

I do.

The water slows long enough for me to see what's floating by—a dead girl.

My hands fly to my mouth.

Bluish-white feet. Tattered hem of a dirty ivory dress. Slashed up arms stretched out like she's on a watery crucifix.

No. It can't be.

Her face. I lean forward, squint.

It is Ha-na.

But then a tiny spider crawls out of her ear. A few more follow.

I rub my eyes.

When I look again, it's not Ha-na. It's not a girl. It's a woman. It's my mom.

19.

I wake up, but the bluish-white feet linger in my mind's eye for a few seconds, crystal clear.

It's dark in my bedroom except for the red digits on my clock. 11:35 p.m. My sheets are soaked.

Ha-na.

Spiders…

Mom.

The nightmare's over. But reality is scary in a different way.

Ha-na won't forgive me. Mom's gone, been gone.

I touch the scab on my inner arm, then touch it two more times.

Check the clock. 11:36 p.m. Check again: 11:36 p.m. I grab my face and turn it away. But no, I have to check again. Still 11:36 p.m.

I really should sleep. I lay back down and close my eyes. Minutes pass.

Can't sleep.

More minutes pass.

I should count.

Get to two hundred one.

This is ridiculous.

I hop out of bed and go to the kitchen for a glass of water.

I consider calling my boys. But what for, this late? To whine about my nightmare? No way. That's my secret.

Peek in Dad's room, he's not there.

I remember what Braid said—that according to In-su's phone conversation with my dad, there's a big "business" deal at the club tonight.

That's where Dad must be. I wish he would've taken me with him. Then maybe I wouldn't have had this bad dream again.

Another time check. 11:45 p.m. *Hmmm.* Dad won't start the deal until 12:30 a.m. *Yeah, yeah, thanks In-su.* Maybe I still have time to make it.

I get dressed quick, then hustle to the underground parking. I have to stop for a second when I see the sleek red body of my car. The Tsukuba red really is the best red, especially with the contrast of the aggressive black and silver rims.

Click-clack. Click-clack.

I look over my shoulder.

An older woman hurries towards the elevator. Her eyes are on my dragon tat. She looks up, and our eyes meet for a second. She drops her head and walks faster.

Whatever.

I slide into the driver's seat, sink in, and start the ignition. I wrap my hands around the leather steering wheel cover. *So smooth*. Each rev of the engine makes my inner smile stretch. Perks.

I fiddle with the stereo to crank up the bass. That's the only way to listen to the Korean hip hop that's on. The entire car vibrates, pushing one of Dad's Marlboro cigs off the dash and onto the passenger seat. I pick it up and sniff. *Not as good as my Dunhills*. I slide his cig, his traitorous cig, into my pocket, thinking about the first time we took a ride together in my car that his TSP "business" money bought.

Bloody-gang-drug money is more like it.

I hunch over and rest my head on the steering wheel. My index finger and thumb clutch the key, I almost turn off the ignition.

Almost. *Fuck it*.

I back up one-handed, then peel out. At first I cruise down the street, but then I push the pedal when I realize I might be late. I maneuver around the few cars that are out.

I reach Itaewon. It's an assortment of boisterous colors—loud yellows and greens in the background and reds, blues, and purples pop up like blaring alarms in the foreground.

I lean my seat back a little more and head nod, pretending I'm in my own music video. Damn! My sweet ride gets me where I'm going before the next bass heavy song is over.

I park a block away from the club because the TSP bouncers would recognize my car. As soon as I step onto the sidewalk, I toss Dad's Marlboro into a trash can and light up a Dunhill. I smoke and walk, keeping my head ducked.

Club Orion's front entrance announces itself with a rowdy crowd of locals, tourists, and G.I.'s. They spill out from the row of gold stanchions connected by red velvet ropes. I turn my head the other way as I pass the bouncers.

I make a right into the next alley. It's narrow and pitch black. I let my fingers skim the concrete wall that's doing a lousy job of containing the thumping bass from inside the club. I shake my head, what a perfect cover for the shit that's about to go down in the back, that hopefully hasn't already gone down.

I get to the fire escape and quick check my pocket watch. 12:34 a.m. I look over my shoulder. All clear. I clamp down on my cig—yank the rusty, creaky iron ladder down, climb to the landing, and hop onto the railing. I balance by grabbing a vertical pipe that's running down the length of the wall. Steady...stretch my free arm. Steady...I grasp the wide-ish ledge, pull myself up in one swift motion, and crouch next to the small window, which I nudge open a crack.

Dad's inside with three of his men. Plastic bags filled with crystal are neatly stacked on a large stainless steel table. Looks like Dad and his men are waiting for the buyers. Dad's eyes are closed, and he's waving his finger like it's a conductor's baton. I listen closer. Yup. The Three Tenors. *Nessun Dorma.*

Three heavy pounds on the door. Dad drops his hand and opens his eyes.

I stub my cigarette on the wall. Check my pocket watch again.

12:38 a.m.

The buyers are late so I figure they're probably American.

Chul-moo looks through the peephole before he unlocks the door and tugs the handle.

Sure enough, two Americans are standing on the other side with anxious grins and poor grooming.

I size them up.

The taller one has dark brown hair in a buzz cut. His uneven stubble and sleepy eyes make him look like one of those hungover American tourists wandering around Itaewon at five in the morning.

The other one has blond hair also in a buzz cut. He looks young, maybe only a few years older than me. He keeps blinking like he has something in his eye. Or is it nerves?

Chul-moo motions for them to enter with his chin, muttering something I can't quite make out.

I lower my head so that my ear is next to the window opening. I want to hear everything.

The blond is carrying an enormous, bulging duffel bag.

In-su straightens his red pocket square. "Pat them down," he instructs in Korean, though he speaks English.

So do my Dad and Chul-moo. I doubt these Americans speak Korean.

Chul-moo frisks the tall one.

The tall one reaches for Chul-moo's red pocket square.

Chul-moo slaps his hand away.

"I was just trying to fix it," the tall one says in English.

And...I was right.

Chul-moo mutters in our mother tongue. "Yeah, of course. You Americans think you can fix everything. Maybe you should try learning my language first."

Hak-kun checks the blond.

The tall one stares at Hak-kun, then nods and smiles. "Love your David Bowie eyes, man," he says.

Yes, Hak-kun has one brown eye and one blue, like David Bowie, but I silent groan and roll my eyes. *We don't all know who David Bowie is! Why should we? Do you know all of our famous singers?*

The tall one turns to Dad and attempts to make small talk. "It's been a hotter spring so far, hasn't it?"

Dad doesn't answer.

He tries again. "Seoul is such a beautiful city. Reminds me of San Francisco. I was there before I got stationed at Yongsan."

Dad ignores him, his face etched in apathy.

My fists clench. When I'm boss, maybe I'll stick to deals with clients from either side of the Korea Strait—other Koreans or Yakuza—because I know they won't try to get all chatty like these Americans. They understand that business boundaries prescribe keeping conversation to a minimum.

The tall one opens his mouth yet again. "Great food too."

I'm out here but still being tortured by this guy's stupid, unnecessary conversation. Wonder how Dad feels. He looks calm and cool.

Dad lights a cigarette, inhales deeply, and blows three smoke rings. "Do we have a deal?" he asks in English.

The tall one's eyes feast on the crystal. "Yes. We'll take it all," he says. He turns to the blond and throws him a chin up. He looks back at Dad. "Here's the money."

The blond steps forward with the bag.

Dad puts one hand up.

The blond stops.

"How much?" Dad asks.

The tall one coughs. "Five, like we agreed on," he says, his voice cracking.

Dad gives a slow stroke to his sideburn with his index finger. He keeps his eyes fixed on the tall one and smiles. "Gentlemen, this meeting is over," Dad says. He switches to Korean and instructs Hak-kun and Chul-moo to show the Americans to the door. He pauses, then adds, "Carve three stars on their chests before you throw them into the alley."

The alley! Oh shit. I gotta get out of here! I prepare to climb down.

A faint smile forms on Chul-moo's lips as he touches his knife. He and Hak-kun bow and walk towards the Americans.

"Wait! Wait!" the tall one cries in a trembling voice.

I wait and look.

Hak-kun and Chul-moo look at Dad. Dad nods. They look back at the Americans.

The tall one swallows unnecessarily. "Did I say five? I meant ten, yay, that's right. Ten."

Dad takes a drag. He doesn't say anything.

Hak-kun shakes his head a little.

Chul-moo smirks as he rolls his shoulders and cracks his neck. Then he punches his tight right fist into his open left palm.

"My friend here is gonna go get the rest from the truck outside," the tall one says pointing at the door with his thumb.

The blond hands the bag to the tall one, then makes for the door, his chin tucked.

"Chul-moo, escort him," Dad says in Korean. "Bring him back if he tries anything funny."

Chul-moo bows and follows the blond to the door. They leave the room.

We wait.

The tall one opens his mouth to say something. But then he gets a load of Dad's irritated expression and shuts it.

Good idea, idiot. Did you really think you'd get away with paying only half? I'd tell your boss about your treachery. Then again, it's your boss' problem if he's got a thief in his lair...

Dad takes one more drag before he stubs his cigarette on the table.

Five minutes later, three heavy pounds on the door.

The blond walks in first, carrying another duffel bag. He gives it to the tall one, who holds both bags out to Dad. "Ten."

Dad looks at Hak-kun and Chul-moo. "Count it," he orders.

They take the duffel bags to a table in the back corner.

The Americans keep their eyes plastered on the concrete floor while

Hak-kun and Chul-moo count the bundles of Benjamins. Dad glares at the Americans. The tension is thick and sticky like the spicy rice cakes I buy at the food cart down the street. The only sound is the shuffling of money bundles.

"Five million," Chul-moo says when he's done.

"Five," Hak-kun confirms.

Dad half smiles. "Looks like we have a deal," he says in English. He holds out his hand for a shake.

The tall one hurries forward. He gives Dad a double handed handshake. "Nice tats," he says, pointing to Dad's hands when he lets go. He whistles, then says, "With tats like that, you must be the boss."

If only this dumbass could see the rest of my dad's ink. He'd shit in his pants.

"Great doing business with you, boss," the tall one says.

That's when Dad lunges forward and punches the verbose a-hole in the gut.

The dude gasps and it looks like his eyes might pop out. He drops to the floor, clutching his belly.

"No one gets away with trying to short me," Dad says in English. Then he kicks the bastard in the flank three times in a row.

I thump my fist once over each of the three blank spaces under my suit. *Don't fuck with TSP.*

Meanwhile Hak-kun and Chul-moo are holding the wild-eyed blond.

Dad lets the tall one writhe on the floor while he goes to the large cabinet at the back.

I go to thump my someday stars again. But my fist freezes when Dad comes back holding up a machete. A wicked shadow passes over Dad's face. He stands over the tall one and raises the machete over his head. His lips curve up into an evil grin. He plunges the blade down fast and hard...

I slam my eyes shut. My fist falls to my side as a wave of nausea hits me. I turn my head away before I dare to open my eyes. I'm not thinking, just moving. I jump onto the fire escape landing, then scurry down the ladder. I sprint down the alley, tripping once. I'm almost to the main street when a tsunami of nausea batters me. I stop and lean forward, pressing my hands onto my knees. Heave...

The congealed contents of my stomach lays in a slimy puddle near the shiny toe caps of my Ferragamo's. I watch my barf spread on the ground, but all I see is the tall one's blood filling the cracks, coagulating.

20.

I rouse from sleep aware that the sheets feel softer. The light trickles in from my window, a blurry delicate gold. I stretch my limbs, then curl up with the covers to soak up the warmth and comfort. The clock reads 7:00 a.m., but time seems gentle and unhurried, like rolling mist. I yawn big, rub my knuckles into my eyes and wait for a second, holding my breath. No raging rivers. No dead Ha-na. No dead Mom.

Maybe those nightmares are over?

I exhale, cautious, tap my nightstand three times, then push the duvet back. More confident, I swing my feet off the bed, jump up, and head to the living room with only the pleasant flashes and echoes of hanging out with my boys yesterday evening. We spent almost six hours at the noraebang mostly singing but also joking, at each other's expense of course. Talking about this and that, nothing in particular. All without a drop of soju, whiskey, or beer. All without a single word about school, our gang stuff, or Ha-na. All without a mention about my dad and his machete. Yeah, I told them about it, and we all agreed that what my dad did was beyond brutal, so terrible in fact that it couldn't be real.

We decided that what I'd seen was actually a horror film disguised as a gangster action film that my dad happened to star in. It's possible. I mean my mom starred in those kinds of films. I've seen them. We've all seen them.

I count the glowing, warm sun rays that stream in from the windows and sliding glass door. Five. They summon me out. Who am I to disregard their luminous call?

A big yawn and stretch as I ease onto the balcony, looking forward to a peaceful view of Seoul as it wakes up. But the patio's a mess. My heart scrambles as I tiptoe around soju bottles and half-full beer glasses strewn in an obstacle course on the tiles. There's an empty bottle of Dad's premium Irish whiskey on the table. An overflowing ashtray that looks like a basket of french fries. A few bowls of spicy peanuts and smoky bacon chips. I pop a chip in my mouth, perfect salty crunch, then I have to chomp down on exactly two more.

I brush the crumbs off the loveseat cushion and plop down. The sunlight drenches my face, assuaging me. My heart beat slows. The gorgeous panorama calls to me, but my dad's open cigarette tin catches my eye. There's one more Marlboro. I reach for it, only because I want to crush it into nothing more than a bunch of grains. My fingers stop short when I see the folded handkerchief next to the tin. My hand changes course, and I lift the soft white cloth. Immediately I recognize its green, single thread border—Mom's handiwork.

The bad guys are coming! Quick hide on the balcony, under the sofa. They won't find you there! I commando crawl under it. Wait with my toy gun at the ready, just in case.

Mom and Dad, not the bad guys, walk out.

Phew! But I stay put and watch.

Mom bows to Dad, holding out a handkerchief with both her hands. "My first successful embroidery is for you," she says. "The willow will keep negative energy away."

Her half smile makes me smile inside. I look at Dad, expecting the same smile. But he isn't smiling, doesn't smile, when he grabs the handkerchief. He runs his finger over the corner. Frowns and says, "This doesn't fix anything. Once a cheater, always a cheater." He crumples Mom's gift and throws it on the tile. It lands in front of my hiding place. The solemn and graceful willow tree that Mom embroidered whispers to me. *It's so sad, Rocky.*

Dad stomps back inside. I peek at Mom. She hangs her head and cries softly. I keep my eyes on Mom as I touch the thread willow.

I weep inside.

I press the handkerchief to my chest. *Dad kept it. That's thoughtful, right?*

The sun grows a little stronger. *Maybe there is hope.*

I skim the cloth over my cheek, then I bring it close to my nose, smell it. I swear I get a faint whiff of Mom's jasmine perfume. I flip it over. The willow tree greets me with its rounded, drooping branches and long, thin leaves. I trace the light green and brown bumpy thread. I unfold it.

What the fuck?

My heart gallops because smack dab in the center is a mysterious lipstick stain. Dark purple.

Definitely not Mom's.

She only wore red. Blood red.

I inspect the imprint of the pair of lips. Touch it. A little rubs off on my finger.

It's fresh. So it was that kind of party, huh, Dad?

He's whistling. I hear him.

I look over my shoulder, Dad's strutting into the kitchen, towel wrapped around his waist, his hair wet. His fierce tats hiss and growl, daring me to step to him. We make eye contact, and he gives me a cocky wink and confident smile. He pours himself some coffee, humming.

I trace the willow tree three times before I lay the handkerchief on my thigh.

Mom made this for you...

I spring up, march inside, glaring at my dad, only he's not my dad. He's just a man. A man who's disrespected my mom. Nothing can stop the words about to shoot out of my mouth.

I slam a fist on the counter. "How could you, Dad?" I accuse, holding up the handkerchief.

He looks up from his coffee. He chuckles, then jokes, "Those aren't my lips."

I don't laugh, I only stare harder. In a gruff voice I say, "They aren't Mom's either."

"So?"

"How could you let some other lady even touch this?"

He doesn't respond. He looks away, sipping his coffee.

I shake the handkerchief at him. "You don't care about Mom, do you?" I drop my eyes and mumble, "I mean you don't even talk about her unless it has to do with me." I whip my head up. "Do you even think about her?"

Another sip. "Of course I think about her," he says, his voice even but his eyes narrowing.

I don't believe him.

The muscles in my face tighten. I lean forward, perfectly composed, and utter three words. "It's truth time." My fuse smolders when I ask, "She was using meth, wasn't she?"

He doesn't say anything.

"Did you even try to stop her? Help her?"

Still nothing except a sip.

By not answering, he's answering all right. "Bet you were glad she was using!" I yell. I glance at the lipstick stain. The thought of Dad with another woman, especially when he's so indifferent about Mom, makes me crazy, and I forget about the crystal. "Why didn't you stop this-this-whoever she was from doing this?"

He sets his coffee mug down, steps forward. "That's enough," he says, tugging at the handkerchief.

I don't let it go. I tighten my hold.

He doesn't let go either. He pulls harder.

My first successful embroidery is for you.

Dad and I stare at each other. Both our faces are stone-cold, but I see red beginning to lace the whites of his eyes.

I up the ante. "You don't love Mom. You never have. Not really. Not the way she loved you." I know I've hit the mark. The veins on his neck jut out and throb.

"Stop. Right now," he says, his voice low and harsh. He comes closer until our faces are a centimeter apart.

"You don't know anything, little boy," he says in a voice as hard as the blade of his machete. "Go run along with your little friends, and do your little things in your little world."

He sounds like Freckle Boy from that night at Bar None. I put Freckle Boy in his place, didn't I?

I give a vicious yank, get the handkerchief away from Dad. I lift my chin. "I know more than you think." I smirk. "I know that you don't follow the TSP code. It's supposed to be an eye for an eye right? But not for you," I say and shake my head. "No. You do what you want. What's good for you," I pause. "I saw what you did to that American buyer. I bet you did the same to the younger one."

Now his breath is a blaze, it burns me like dragon fire.

"Are you proud?" I ask. "Are you proud you're a killer, proud you—"

He cuts me off. "I kill people who fuck me over!" he screams, jabbing my chest with his fist. He gives me a creepy look. "I kill people who fuck me over," he says again but this time in a quieter, sinister voice. He leans in so that our noses graze, and his woody aftershave tries to exile me in a remote cedar forest. "Anyone who fucks me over," he snarls.

I scoff. "I bet you do. Did Younger Uncle fuck you over? Maybe you didn't banish him. Maybe you killed him?"

Dad's face gets white, not the pale, frightened ghost white but the scorching, enraged white. His entire body stiffens.

"You killed him, didn't you?"

Next thing I know, Dad's fist smashes my face.

21.

I'm in that confusing place between sleep and wakefulness, where my mind yawns and stretches but my body won't move. I try to open my eyes...can't.

But my mind's eye flies open. Mom appears in a spotlight's beam, her expression wistful.

She glides over and sits on the edge of my bed. She strokes my sixteen-year-old forehead the way she did when I was a kid, smiles at me with her eyes and lips.

An angel.

"How about a story before you dream your own?" she whispers.

I nod.

"Our favorite?"

I nod. The first time she told me this Korean myth she showed me a faded photo of her and her mother sitting under an enormous willow tree.

"My father took this photo near our house." She let out a slow breath. "The willow's branches were bent and posed in impossible ways, and it seemed to cry so many long green tears. On this quiet afternoon, my parents and I sat under it, resting our heads on the trunk. The sun filtered down through the lush canopy, a soft glow. I almost fell asleep, but then my mother spoke. 'No matter what we lose, we can't give up,' she said. Then she patted the brittle bark. 'Like this willow, all those years of drought, and it kept fighting to survive. Now look it at. It's thriving.' She looked at me and smiled. 'Did I ever tell you the story of Yuhwa, the goddess of the willow tree?' I shook my head."

Mom grazes my cheek with her knuckle, then she sits up straight. She clasps her hands on her crossed knees and clears her throat in the most delicate way possible before she begins. "Yuhwa was the goddess of the willow tree..."

I smile inside, picturing the same pretty lady in an elegant willow tree. She looks like my mom. Her long, brown skirt blends in with the bark. Her green top with billowy sleeves flows into the draping branches. The wind blows a sad song, and she and the willow weep a little.

"She was the eldest of three daughters of the river god, Habaek. She was beautiful, intelligent, and kind. One day the sun god, Haemosu, captured her. He wanted her to be his bride. Habaek was angry. How dare Haemosu try to marry his daughter without asking him for permission?"

I nod, my eyes solemn.

"Habaek ordered Haemosu to come to his palace to discuss the matter. Do you know what happened, my darling?"

I shake my head.

"Boys will be boys," she says with a despondent laugh.

I rub my sleepy eyes.

"Rocky, shall I finish the story tomorrow?"

I want to shake my head but it drops, as do my eyelids. No matter. I already know how it ends.

Haemosu showed up in the form of a sunbeam and got her pregnant. She bore his son, Jumong…

I open my left eye just as the first apricot rays burst over the Han, like the soft petals of a pale orange rose blooming. I drag my legs off the bench and sit up, wincing at the sudden sharp pain in my right eye. I touch it gently. A big bouncy eye blister touches back…

Dad's punch. Running out of the penthouse. Refuge in the arms of Seoul. Walking, walking, walking the streets. All day. All night.

I reach for my knife. It's there. I trace my stars, my name.

I check my pocket watch. 5:47 a.m. Yawn. I stand and press my hands into my back to stretch my hips forward. I straighten up, do a few twists. There's no one around, but as I corkscrew my upper body to the left one last time, my good eye lands on a flash of red. I squint. It's a black suit with a red pocket square behind a thick tree trunk. The face is blurry.

What the heck?

I blink, rub my left eye, and look again. It's only a tree. I guess I'm more exhausted than I feel. I'm seeing things.

I inspect the tree—it's a willow. A breeze comes and, when the willow sways, I imagine it's a sorrowful and lonely Yuhwa.

I look at the Han, resting my hand on the empty half of the bench next to me. The wooden slats are so cold...

I close my left eye and pretend I'm not alone.

Who did this to you, Rocky my darling?

Dad.

How could he? Oh, my sweet boy, let me take a look...

Open my eye.

My fingers skim my sore eye.

Touch my good eye, then bad eye, then good eye again.

I light up a Dunhill, take a long drag, and exhale, trying to let out more than the smoke.

It doesn't work.

Smoke to forget, but get lost in regret.

I realize I'm clutching the Dunhill tin, staring at Mom in the wedding photo. I slam it shut and shove it into my inner jacket pocket. I suck the smoke deep into my lungs and keep it trapped in there, not caring how my lungs feel.

I hate you both!

No, I don't.

Yes, I do.

No...

When I finally release, it's messy like the hazy aftermath of a recently extinguished fire.

I think about another photo, our family photo by the lovelocks.

Wish I hadn't destroyed it.

I close my left eye and picture the gochujang red lovelock.

I should find it.

The idea flutters around in my mind.

I should find it.

The idea sticks, but way too hard. It makes me explode off the bench, stub my cig before it's even a quarter done. I dump it in the trash and start marching towards Namsan Seoul Tower. When I reach a main sidewalk, I take care to step over the cracks.

I arrive at the bottom of the hill, take a deep breath, preparing for the stairs. I start out fast and count each step as I go. Six hundred forty-nine. It's practically summer, but the Christmas feeling hits me as soon as both my feet plant on the Roof Terrace, the same way it did the day of the photo and many days before that.

Warmth and merriment. Candy and raised glasses...

I smile inside as I walk the length of the fence to where we stood all those years ago. There are so many more love locks. At first only my left eye searches. No luck. I dive in with both hands.

Just when I think I won't find it, I do. It's under a large black lovelock with a silver skull and crossbones.

I inspect my family's lovelock. Our names written in black ink are long gone. But I know it's ours for sure because of the three small scratches on one side from when I dropped it. I tap each scratch, then stand there holding the lovelock. I tap it again. Cradle it. Tap it once more.

A gentle scraping behind me.

I look over my shoulder. There's a middle-aged maintenance man behind me. His face is blank, and he's holding a broom slightly off the ground like he's in mid-sweep. We exchange glances. He looks away and resumes sweeping.

I turn back to the fence but begin to wobble. I'm exhausted, hardly able to reach a nearby bench before my legs give out. I plop down, then close my eye and let my head droop.

I'm a piece of shit.

Footsteps. Giggles.

I lift my head, open my eye.

A family of three strolls along the fence. The parents are arm-in-arm, and there's a stainless steel lovelock hooked on the mother's pinky finger. The kid runs ahead, trips, and falls splat on the planks. He peels himself up, then sits clutching one of his knees. A fresh layer of blood oozes from a small abrasion. His parents sprint over and drop to his side.

I start to yawn but shut my mouth quick because of what I see next. Or rather, who I see.

Ha-na!

She's got a sketchbook tucked under her arm and a pencil on her ear. She doesn't see me as she walks past. She sits on the next bench over. For a few seconds she watches the parents tend to their kid. Then she flips open her sketchbook, plucks her pencil, and starts drawing big lines. She looks back and forth between the family and her blank page, drawing and shading.

I check her arms. But I can't see even a hint of her scars because her long sleeves are past her wrists.

The parents help the kid up. The mother gives him the lovelock. He hobbles over to the fence and snaps it in place. They each take turns saying a few words. One selfie and group hug later their little ceremony is done. They walk back the way they came.

Ha-na turns her head to follow them, and that's when she sees me. Her eyes widen, but then she narrows them and frowns. She looks away, slamming her sketchbook shut. She slides her pencil over her ear and shoots up. She takes long-legged strides all the way to the stairs.

She's booking it down when my mouth opens. "Ha-na! Wait up!"

She doesn't. Why would she?

I catch up to her and slow down so that our steps are in sync. "Ha-na."

She stops. Looks at me with a blank face.

"I just want to tal—"

She cuts me off. She's staring at my right eye. "What happened?"

"Oh this?" I scramble for a face-saving explanation. "Got in a fight. It's no big deal."

She squints at me. "Does it hurt?"

I nod.

She touches her arm, and I swear she's smiling a slight half smile.

Damn. An eye for an eye.

Her fingers drift under her long sleeve.

I'm a piece of shit.

I focus on the ground around my feet, count the little pebbles until I get to a safe seven. Then I fix a serious eye on her. "Maybe your parents want to make my eyes equal?" I ask.

Her eyes meet my left eye and harden. She drops her free arm and tightens her hold on her sketchbook. But then her unrelenting stare softens, and her eyes become open wounds that bleed. She rubs them dry, her expression back to unreadable. "My parents don't know there's anything to make equal. They don't know…" She inhales sharply before letting out a slow breath. In a flat voice she says, "My parents see my future, not me."

Now there's something I wasn't expecting her to say, not in a million years.

My dad doesn't see me either…

But I don't say it. It doesn't seem fair that I vent to her. Me, the bully. I don't think I have that right.

Ha-na tucks her chin, and her pencil dives off the springboard of her ear. It lands on a step and rolls. We both bend down. Our hands reach for it at the same time. Her sleeve pulls up at the wrist.

She grabs the pencil first, then glances at me.

My good eye is already homed in on her scars.

She flings her arm so that her sleeve barrels back down, then she launches up to a stand.

I stand, slower. Smooth my suit.

She spins her pencil around her thumb.

I count the spins.

On number four (*four*!), she stops. She holds the pencil close to her body with both hands. She's gripping each end so tight her hands shake a little. The pencil snaps and so does she.

"Whatever," she grumbles, "I don't cut anymore." She glares at me, pulling her shoulders back to stand taller. "I'm done hurting myself because of assholes like you. Go ahead and harass me. I don't even care if the entire school keeps doing it next year. I only have one more year to go in this hell hole before I'm out of here. My parents won't like it. But I'll be moving onto bigger and better things than all of you pathetic bully losers with nothing better to do than kick people when they're down."

I'm speechless. *A pathetic bully loser...*

22.

Dad stomps out of the penthouse without one word to me, slamming the front door shut like an angry exclamation point. It must be in bold and italics. I'm sure it punctuates a long and very thorough string of profanity. I'm hunched over in the living room, hands in my pockets—my body literally a question mark to an ongoing mental inquiry. *Why would you punch me? Why are you such a traitor to the TSP code? Why why why?*

My chest burns.

But guess what, Dad?

I straighten up into my own pissed-off exclamation point, only I'm making a quiet declaration with mine.

I'll have my eye for an an eye.

I light up a Dunhill and smoke it fast and hard, pacing. I ash my cig on the spotless hardwood floor as I go because, hey, trashing Dad's little castle just about covers my eye. I thrust the glowing end of the butt on the wall and twist, smiling inside at the burn mark it leaves on the ivory paint. I let it fall and immediately grab a nearby glass vase. I toss and catch it a few times, then grip it tight and draw my arm back.

But I can't throw it like I want to because Ha-na pops into my head, and I suddenly feel ridiculous.

I set the vase down, take three deep belly breaths of the silent and still penthouse air. I touch my tiger tat, my dragon, and then my tiger again. I prowl the penthouse, mostly because I don't know what else to do with myself. So, yup, I'm a tiger. I get fully into character, like Mom used to do when she was rehearsing. I prowl. And I hunt.

I end up in Dad's den, ready to strike. I canvass his territory, low growl as I slink past and touch all the artifacts of his bachelor bosshood. Rows and rows of neatly lined books. A mini-bar with bottles of all shapes and sizes. His collection of rare and costly whiskey and cognac. My fingers touch the level mark of the liquid in each dark, translucent bottle. An antique globe next, I spin it. Then a glass display case with ancient weapons and a few torture devices.

I get to Dad's desk and pounce onto his oversized leather chair, knees first. It swivels. I make it swivel more. Three times. Then I recline with my feet crossed on his desk. I touch my face, another of Dad's relics—the face his double-crossing fist smashed in. It doesn't hurt as much anymore.

There's a stainless steel pocket flask next to his desk lamp. I snatch it and inspect my eye on its polished surface—the big ass blister has transformed into a sloppy, colorful mess. Like a five-year-old drew a green circle, then fingerpainted a bunch of purple and blue inside, sort of staying in the line.

I bring the flask closer to my eye. Trace the purple parts of my bruise...

Dad did this.

I think of Mom.

She used to say she was still wearing makeup from a fight scene in the movie she'd done earlier that day.

Messy makeup is an easy pill to swallow when you're a little kid, much easier than a serrated your-family-is-totally-fucked-up one. Makes sense that I grew up addicted to it. Well, it does to me, I mean don't all kids want to believe more than anything that their family is okay?

I hold my palms open, imagining a smooth capsule in the left and a spiky one in the right. I can't pull my eyes away from my right hand. I bring it to my mouth…

It wasn't makeup, it was…

I swallow it. It hurts going down, like a thousand needles piercing my throat.

Dad beat Mom.

I toss the flask over my shoulder, it lands on the chair. I wrap my hands around the edge of the desk. There's an official-looking document under my right hand. My fingers rake the sheet towards me. I crumple it into a tight wad.

Dad beat Mom!

I shut my eyes and press my palms onto my ears, shaking my head. No! Bury it again!

Dad beat Mom!

I can't, and I'm breathing faster. I touch my injured eye with my index finger. Press it. Hard. Harder. Harder still. A sharp pain sends a shock wave through my body. But it's not as bad as the knowledge that my own Dad could do such a thing to Mom and me.

My cell vibrates. It's a text from Braid, the tenth today. *Hello?*

I ignore it like I've ignored all nine others. And the five each from Strike and Patch.

Maybe I should stop being such a hermit. Maybe I should tell them what happened.

Maybe...I should...blah blah blah.

I seize a heavy paperweight and hurl it. It slams into the sliver of wall between two bookcases, leaves a cracked dent, and lands on the floor with a thud. Something from the top of the right bookcase drops to the floor, a slightly more muffled thud.

I look.

It's actually two things. A black velvet pouch and a small white envelope.

I cross the room in a fog, stand over the fallen items, chin tucked. The envelope is addressed to my dad, but I don't recognize the return address.

1233-33 Yeonhwa-ri, Baengnyeong-myeon, Ongjin-gun, Incheon, South Korea.

Postmarked...I do the math...ten years ago. I pick it up and have a look inside. No letter, no nothing. I stuff the envelope into my pocket and scoop up the pouch. It's weighty. I untie the satin ribbons at the top. Peek inside. There's a tangle of a gleaming gold chain. I lift it. My eyes bulge at what's on the end of the chain—one of the TSP medallions I've been coveting. It winks at me with all its diamond eyes. Without thinking I put the necklace on. It feels more like a neck shackle than boss jewelry, but I keep it on. I lift the medallion and tuck it inside my shirt, letting the metal brand my skin with cold.

Whose is it? Not Dad's. He never takes his off. It's probably Older Uncle's, the one I tried to snag from his portrait when I was younger.

Good hiding place, Dad.

I stand on my tiptoes and slide the empty pouch back on top of the bookshelf. I reach into my pocket for the envelope, read the return address again. *Who sent Dad a letter from Baengnyeong Island? What did the letter say?*

I go to put the envelope back on the bookshelf, but I stop and stare at it. Baengnyeong Island. From what I know, Dad and his brothers were born and raised there. It's one of a group of remote islands in the Yellow Sea that makes up Ongjin county, and it's a four-hour boat ride from its mother city of Incheon. It's actually closer to North Korea than South.

Dad told me that growing up, his parents made him and his brothers study Christianity in the hopes that they would someday become good Christian ministers like their father. But there were rumors that behind closed doors, their father practiced extreme discipline methods. Often without reason. And so the Yi brothers spent their time gallivanting around the island doing anything to avoid their father and "the good Christian life." Eventually they learned that the monetary fruits of being a Christian minister were few, and they weren't interested in spiritual fruits. So instead they dabbled in gambling. To their surprise, it paid off bigtime. Aspirations for greater wealth lured them into other sinful pursuits…

Yi Nam-il, Older Uncle. Yi Dae-sung, Dad. Yi Man-sik, Younger Uncle. Three Yi brothers. Three Star Pa.

I stuff the envelope in my pocket and light up. I pace and rapid smoke, pressing the medallion against my chest. This time it scorches.

I kill people who fuck me over! Anyone who fucks me over.

I touch my bruised eye, then my cheek. *Dad's a loose cannon.*

I have so many questions. Years of questions…

I read the return address again.

1233-33 Yeonhwa-ri, Baengnyeong-myeon, Ongjin-gun, Incheon, South Korea.

Who sent this from the island? What was it?

Maybe it's only a weird coincidence.

No more questions!

I slip the envelope under the pouch and push both a little further back on the top of the bookshelf. I head out of the den. But I stop at the door. I can't walk out, not yet. I press the medallion against my chest once more. *No doubt the envelope was with it for a reason.* I pivot, zip to the shelf, and retrieve it. I trace the return address.

My dad and uncles and grandparents are from the island. My grandparents died years ago, but maybe I have other relatives there as well?

My roots.

A flutter in my belly becomes a hungry spasm.

Who sent this from the island? What was it?

Whoever, whatever, I need to know. I have to know.

I have to go to the island. I've been wanting answers, and this could be a start.

My skin prickles. I tap the medallion three times before pulling out my cell and sending a group text.

Pack your bags, boys...

23.

The ferry glides over the ocean, over all the different blues that could spill from a box of colored pencils. The panorama of the sky and horizon offer even more. Every shade of the rich primary color stretches and blends in front of me. But four unlucky blues dominate—cobalt, denim, baby, and teal.

I take a deep breath of the cool, salty air and light up a faithful Dunhill to forget the chromatic misfortune. I close my eyes when I take my first soothing drag. Open and release a smokey stream.

Better.

But then the ferry rams through an unexpected set of choppy waves and I stumble, almost dropping my cig. I grab the railing for balance, holding the cig close to my chest until we're over the last rough peak.

Soon everything is calm and steady again. I take a long draw, tilt my head back, and exhale a cloud into the cloudless sky.

Mom used to say a plain blue sky, even if it's the most gorgeous azure or cerulean, is boring. A silvery cloud or two makes the perfect sky more like real life—imperfect.

Imperfect.

Everyone's imperfect. Everything's imperfect.

I stare back at the ocean, at the billions of drops, the drops that become waves.

A wild wind sweeps over the water's surface.

I'm a drop, Mom's the wind. She left me behind, and I'm waiting for her to rush back over me, form me into a wave so I can travel faster. Maybe catch up with her...

A tap on the shoulder. I turn.

"Excuse me," a young foreigner says in Korean, lowering his heavy backpack onto the deck. He rakes his fingers through his blond hair, then hunches over a pocket-size book, *Basic Korean Phrases*. He lifts his head and asks in broken Korean, "Do you have a cigarette, please?"

Not bad. I pull out my tin, hold it open for him.

He takes a cig and puts it between his dry, cracked lips. He pats his pockets, then shrugs.

I offer him a light, which he accepts with a grateful smile. He takes a few short draws until it's lit. "Gamsahamnida," he says.

I nod.

He faces the ocean and sucks the smoke deep into his lungs. He exhales, then grins so big I think maybe it's his first smoke in a few days.

For a couple of quiet minutes, we both gaze out at the glistening water, enjoying our Dunhills.

Halfway through his cig, he whips out his phrasebook, runs his finger down a page, and asks "Sorry, do you speak English?"

"Yes," I answer in English.

"What's on the island for you?" he asks in American English.

"Answers. I hope."

He raises an eyebrow but doesn't say anything at first. Another couple of inhales and exhales before he says, "Cool."

"And you?" I ask, glad to have this opportunity to practice speaking another language.

"I want to check out the rock formations at Dumujin," he says. He flicks his wrist about as he talks. "Oh, and, you know, it's the frontline. What's that like, right?" He smiles, it's a nervous smile.

"I was wondering that myself," I say, trying to imagine being only seventeen kilometers away from North Korea all the time, being able to see the North Korean coastline on a clear day...

I shudder inside.

The American finishes his cig. He thanks me one more time, then hoists his backpack onto his shoulder. One warm smile and chin up later he heads below deck.

The wind picks up, forcing the waves to do the same. A spray of cold sea. I shiver. *Fuck this*. Time to go inside.

My boys are chilling in a corner booth, devouring chocolate-glazed donuts and playing a card game—Mighty. I slide in next to Braid.

"We'll deal you in next round, boss," he says over the loud constant drone of chattering and the engine.

I nod. I look around at the crowd of mostly mainland Seoulites and some Europeans, Americans, and Japanese. What's on Baengnyeong Island for all these people?

There are also five ROK marines in camo. Their faces are as stone-cold as mine.

I thought Dad and his TSP gangsters were badass…

My eyes trace the Republic of Korea flag patch that's stitched onto one of their sleeves. I pull my slouching shoulders back to sit taller. The dangerous border zone seems a little less dangerous with these bad boys nearby. And if the Democratic People's Republic of Korea changes its mind about the armistice agreement today, at least there will be five more of our marines on the island.

A touch of my brow, my subtle salute of respect and thanks to the ROK marines.

Then I look back at my boys, clasp my hands on the table, and watch them play.

Suddenly Strike's eyes get huge. He clutches his belly and blurts, "Oh shit!" He grabs a barf bag just in time because all at once he gags and vomits. When he's done, he wipes his mouth. "Never been on a boat," he says folding the top of the bag.

Patch slaps him on the back, shaking his head. He chuckles silently.

Strike picks up his cards. "Where were we?" he asks. But then he heaves one more time. He rips open the bag and pukes again. With his chin still tucked, he asks, "Remind me again, boss, why we're going to this far, far island?"

I know he doesn't mean anything by it, but it hits a nerve. I glare at him.

His smile fades. He moves his jaw to the side.

Braid scoffs and kicks him under the table hard enough that we all hear it. "You're such a dumbass," he says.

"What?" Strike asks, crumpling the top of the bag, then dropping it under the table. He shrugs, palms out. "I'm joking around!"

Braid and Patch frown at Strike.

Strike stares at the table. "Sorry, boss. I just hope"—he stops and presses his fist onto his lips and holds his other hand up. He waits a few seconds like that. The nausea seems to pass because he lowers his hands—"just hope it's worth it."

24.

The pier juts out, desolate, into the cold waves. Above, gulls swoop and caw. I step onto the aging wooden planks splattered with dark bull's-eyes in white, my senses naked without all the traffic, construction, and skyscrapers of Seoul. The Baengnyeong sun feels heavier, the breeze briny and sharp. I take a deep breath. A whiff of pungent sea, like cured fish. In the distance there are thickets of spruce trees. I imagine weaving, quiet, through the trunks, coming out onto a deserted beach.

But the tranquil beauty that welcomes us is only half the story. There are also barbed wire fences and a line of ROK marines standing at attention. Not to mention the distant whistling of artillery fire. Is there anything more extreme than the sights and sounds of the persistent North Korean threat?

My boys disembark. We stand shoulder to shoulder with nothing to hide behind. The marines greet their comrades with sharp salutes, about-face, and march in formation. We follow them, from a respectful distance of course, down the long pier, our apprehension cloaked in our exaggerated swagger. We don't speak.

When they're out of sight, we relax. Walk looser.

Strike shoves Patch. "Hey big boy, go crouch over there," he says pointing in front of us. He rubs his hands together. "Leapfrog time!"

Patch jogs over and bends forward at the waist, pressing his hands onto his legs below his knees so that his back is flat.

Strike looks at me. "Ready, boss?"

I give a chin up.

He dashes towards Patch, then vaults over, his legs spread eagle. He lands steady on his feet and quick turns to me, grinning. He stretches out his arms, bows. "What do you think?" he asks, not waiting for me to answer before he looks at Patch. "Your turn, big boy."

The two of them take turns the length of the pier, the way we used to across the courtyard at school. Back then it was as kids in our uniforms, today it's as teenagers in fancy suits. I smile inside.

Strike misses his next landing and wipes out hard. But he jumps up fast, like it's nothing because it really is nothing for Mr. Grandmaster. "I'm ok!" he shouts, brushing off his suit.

Braid and I catch up. There's a red line on Strike's chin.

I point to it. "You're bleeding."

Strike touches the cut and looks at the red smear on his finger. "So I am." He looks back at me. "It's what I get for questioning you, boss."

An eye for an eye. My boy.

I grab a cig. So do my boys. We walk and smoke all cool with each other the rest of the way to the car rental.

Braid drives us. We decide to stop in Jinchon-ri for a quick lunch. He parks, and we step out into the small town, our appetites piqued.

No one else is around. A forlorn wind rushes by. It's silent and eerie, a ghost town that reminds me of Nolda Land. We stroll down the narrow, uneven sidewalk lined with a few rusty cars.

All the buildings are one or two stories. We pass by a coffee shop and two family restaurants. A karaoke bar. An admin building. Convenience store. A church. A funky-looking dive restaurant. A gas station.

We settle on the dive because the sign in the window says they only serve buckwheat dumplings, a local speciality. It turns out to be a tasty choice.

Stomachs full, it's road trip time. We head east, north, then west. Every kilometer of the scenic drive is a strange juxtaposition of conflict and peace. The pristine north facing beaches are all blocked off by high razor wire fences. A couple of marines jog towards us. They hop onto the grassy shoulder, trampling over purple wildflowers.

No other cars on the road. Ahead, soaring pine trees...

I'm tired. My eyes start to close, but then the car hits a pothole. I'm wide awake. I crank down my window for some fresh air, poke my head out a little. The breeze refreshes me like a cold shower on a steamy day. The turbulent ocean with all its agitated whitecaps is mesmerizing.

I reach into my outer jacket pocket for the envelope. It's wrinkled, and I smooth it out on my lap. I trace the return address. *1233-33 Yeonhwa-ri, Baengnyeong-myeon, Ongjin-gun, Incheon, South Korea.*

Strike's dangling his entire head and both arms out of his window. He pulls himself back in, claps, and says, "Alright boys, it's game time."

Braid groans.

Strike cranes his neck for a better look at the sky. Then he punches Patch in the arm. "Every time you see one of those birds," he says pointing to an elegant Chinese egret, "you're allowed to punch the guy next to you." He holds up a finger. "But, if it's a false alarm, he gets to punch you back. Harder."

"Brilliant," Braid mumbles.

The Chinese egret's white plumage gleams in the blue sky. I can't help but marvel at its long wingspan and strong flight.

Meanwhile Patch punches Strike.

"That's a false alarm, buddy," Strikes says and goes to punch back.

Patch grabs Strike's fist, then points to the same egret.

Strike shakes his head. "No dummy, it has to be a different one."

Patch is silently cracking up.

"Hey! You knew that. You just wanted to punch me!" Strike fake whines.

My backseat boys point and punch, but Braid and I can't be bothered. We keep our eyes on the open road. I don't know what Braid's thinking, but I'm lost counting the center dashes as my hopes, expectations, and fears compete for attention.

We arrive. Yeonhwa-ri. I check the map on my cell.

"Turn left up there," I say.

"You got it, boss," Braid says.

We pull up in front of a small white house with green trim. 1233-33. It's got a tiny, well-manicured front yard. There's no car parked in the driveway. The curtains are drawn. Everything is still and quiet.

"Wait here." I jump out of the car, then up the two steps to the door. I knock three times. Wait. No answer. Knock three more times. Wait. Still no answer. I walk around the side of the house to the back. Knock on the door there. Nothing.

"We'll try again later," I tell my boys. "Let's drive."

Braid nods and pulls out onto the empty road.

I light up a cig, inhale nice and slow, and exhale a smoky pattern that reminds me of large boulders. I wonder if the American made it to the cliffs. They looked magnificent in the tourist brochures back at the car rental. "Let's check out Dumujin," I say.

We get there just as a tour van full of mainlanders departs.

Braid parks. "Glad we missed that zoo."

Strike slams the door behind him. He tilts his head back to examine the sky. "I say we're still allowed to punch if we see a—"

Braid cuts him off. "No."

Strike crosses his arms and drops his shoulders in a sulk. "Whatever."

We get to a decked walkway. Huge stunning rocks jut out of the sea. Gusts whisper secrets in a language we can't understand. The ocean glints here and there in the splendid sunshine as if it's winking a morse code message.

Dumujin. A fitting name. The enormous rock formations do look like broad-shouldered, brave generals putting their heads together for a discussion. I can't help but imagine my boys and me doing the same thing someday when we lead TSP.

A flock of gulls beat their wings and wheel overhead like they own the sky. The sea roars and crashes into the cliffs, sending white, salty spray that we breathe in.

Braid leans over the wooden railing, points to the ocean. "Bet it would look even more awesome from out there," he yells loud enough to cut through the pounding waves. "Let's hire a boat next time?"

We approach the end of the walkway. That's when I see a man standing with his back to us. His elbows are propped on the railing and his fingers are interlaced behind his head. The ends of his shoulder-length black hair blow about in the vigorous wind.

His hands...

On the man's right—a ferocious black tiger surrounded by flames, its eyes glowing orange. Left—a fierce red dragon breathing fire on a black heart.

25.

Scant clouds drift our way, a few raindrops sprinkle. The man looks
at the sky, holding out his palm. Then he stuffs his tatted hands into
the pockets of his jeans. His orange and black North Face windbreaker
flutters in a gust. He rocks back and forth on his heels.

He turns around. *His face.*

With his dark, crusty hard skin, three day stubble, and crows feet,
he's a taller, weathered version of my dad. Of me, even.

Younger Uncle strolls towards us in a slight leanback. Neck down,
he's the opposite of a smooth, slick city gangster. He looks like a rugged
outdoorsman.

A huge wave pummels the rocks.

He doesn't say anything. Another wave washes over the rocks and
along with it a sense of familiarity washes over me. *His vibe…*

Besides my dad and me, I didn't think anyone else had that intense
yet calm and in control vibe. Older Uncle didn't. He was jolly.

Our eyes connect, mirroring each other with their icy cold blackness.

A shiver down my spine, but I play all cool.

When he stops in front of me, I bow.

He glances at my hands. Then he holds out his hand for a shake, his expression stoic. We shake hard. It's a strange thing—shaking hands with someone who could be your future self.

He says, his gruff voice matching his unrefined demeanor, "The last time I saw you, you shot me with your gun." Then he winks. "Your toy gun," he adds with a chuckle.

My mouth is dry. I don't know what to say, so I don't say anything. I count the lines on his face instead.

"Yi Kyung-seok," he says reaching for my shoulder. "It's been way too long." He pulls me in for a hug.

I don't lift my arms. I stand there like a statue while he embraces me. *This has happened before...*

He let's go and pats my shoulders. "Rocky..." he says, letting his voice trail off. He smiles. "Your mother certainly picked the perfect nickname for you. You haven't even blinked." He pauses, rubs his chin with his index finger and thumb as he studies my face. He shifts in place and widens his stance, crossing his arms high and tight.

I still don't speak or move.

He draws his face back, raises an eyebrow, and says, "I'm an extremely busy man. Are you going to talk or what?"

Strike snickers. I flash him a dirty look.

My flesh and blood is standing before me, but I can't think of a single thing to say.

His expression softens. "So who are your friends?" he asks.

"This is Braid," I say pointing with my chin to the right. Then to the left. "This is Strike. And that's Patch."

My boys bow.

He offers each of them a shake, grinning. He looks back at me. "You boys hungry?" he asks.

We all nod.

26.

Rain hammers the roof of the rundown restaurant with a vengeance, like it wants to break through the shingles and wash us off the face of the earth. But I stop hearing it when the unmistakable aroma of gimchi calls to me. I inhale deeply, the scent is a little milder, a little sweeter than the Seoul versions I'm used to. Younger Uncle, my boys, and I head to a tiny table near a large window and settle down. A group of marines—seven of them—are scarfing down their meals one table over, and suddenly I don't feel so tough anymore. These ROK marines in their stiffly starched uniforms embody a stalwartness I can't imagine possessing, but I'd never admit that to anyone. I touch my knife, trace my stars, my name, as my eyes trace their standard-issue assault rifles.

A server takes our order, then scurries into the kitchen.

The screen door creaks open. An elderly couple hobbles in. The old man's hands tremble as he closes an oversized umbrella and props it against the door. They go straight to a table at the back. Maybe that's their table, their perk: no intimidation required. I doubt the old man in his faded t-shirt and slippers is a boss.

Younger Uncle watches the old man help his wife sit down. "This place used to be packed with locals and tourists," he says. He drapes one arm over the back of his chair and pivots his body towards the marines. He points to them with his chin, says, "You see more of them out and about these days. The military wants to reassure everyone that things are all good. Especially after the crisis last week..."

"Crisis?" Then I remember what the guy on the nightly news said. "You mean the ROK naval patrol ship that disappeared?"

Younger Uncle nods. "It's still a mystery, but everyone around here thinks North Korea sunk it. It wouldn't be the first time."

I glance at the marines, grateful for their amphibious training. *We're safe from an attack...*

Our naengmyeon arrives. My boys attack their noodles, slurping the long strands and the frigid broth.

I take a bite. I like the chewy texture of the sweet potato starch. And the broth isn't salty or meaty. It's subtle. Refreshing. Pure and clean.

Younger Uncle stirs his soup with his chopsticks. "Seems like the North doesn't follow an eye for an eye," he mumbles.

"Eye for an eye?" I ask, taken aback for a second that he's not talking about TSP.

"The law of retaliation," he says. "You shouldn't injure another person more than they've done to you. It should be the same or less."

I nod, thinking about Dad, not North Korea. "You mean like the TSP code," I say straining to keep my voice even. "My dad doesn't follow it either."

Strike swallows his bite. "Does that make your dad like...North Korea?"

Younger Uncle almost chokes on his sip of water. He coughs, thumping his fist on his chest. He adjusts himself on his chair. "I meant more like the way South Korea is approaching the conflict. The military is setting up a special forces brigade—an "amputation unit"—to send a powerful message to the North Korean leaders. But they won't actually cut off anyone's body parts." He stops, gulps some water. "Unless of course the North hurts or kills one of our leaders. Then I'm thinking it's an eye for an eye. An arm for an arm. A head for a head."

"Makes sense," Braid mumbles, his mouth full of noodles.

I'm still stuck on my dad and TSP's code. I open my mouth to bring it up again, but Younger Uncle speaks first.

"Wish we could all get along," he says, releasing a slow breath. He lifts some of the noodles with his chopsticks and stares at them. "This particular naengmyeon is a classic North Korean dish." He releases the noodles. "The owner of this restaurant is from there. Defected to the island years ago." He stirs the soup. "He told me this is an old family recipe. The secret is the sand lance fish sauce. In his village up north, it was mostly the elderly that ate this." He pauses to suck down some noodles and broth. Shakes his head, smiling. "His recipe amazes me. See, after the war, this style spread to the island, then Incheon, and eventually Seoul and the rest of the peninsula. Soon everyone, north and south, young and old, was enjoying this dish." He takes a big bite, chews, and swallows. "The noodles connect us all. We're not that different." He lays his chopsticks down and interlaces his fingers on the table. "The problem isn't most people North or South. It's some of the leaders, they're just like a gang. Only thinking of themselves and how they can gain wealth and power. How they can hold onto it."

I nod. My thoughts roam free on the open plain of Younger Uncle's words. *The problem isn't Ha-na, it never was. She never was. The problem is my mini-TSP gang and especially me as the boss.*

I think about my dad.

The problem isn't most people in Seoul, it's TSP and especially my dad and uncles as the bosses.

Younger Uncle turns to Patch, slaps his back. "Good?"

Patch nods vigorously. He pats his belly and shows Younger Uncle his empty bowl.

Younger Uncle looks at Braid and Strike. They're done too.

"It was delicious," Braid says, licking his lips.

Strike, with his sleepy eyes and satisfied smile, slides down in his chair. The boys relax while Younger Uncle and I finish up.

After his last bite, Younger Uncle tucks his long hair behind his ears. He looks at me. "You know, Rocky, I knew it was you even before I turned around."

"How?" I ask.

"I felt it in my bones," he says with a serious expression.

"You felt it in your bones? Yeah?"

He nods once before leaning back with his hands behind his head. "It started early this morning when the sky was red. I stood in my yard, the same way I do every morning, and let my bare feet sink into the dewy grass. I pushed my hands into my hips, closed my eyes, and took a deep breath. But when I opened I felt an ache in my knees and shoulders. A little while later it started to rain." He smiles at me. "My bones told me today was going to be special. Something important was going to happen. All I could think was maybe my biggest wish, to see you again, would come true. Then I heard footsteps on the walkway. I felt a few raindrops and got a twinge in my bones…"

I suck down the last few drops of the precious broth and cross my arms tight, shaking my head. "Sounds like you have arthritis, and it was flaring up. That's what happens to some people with the pressure changes in the weather right before rain—they feel it in their bones alright."

Everyone laughs.

Younger Uncle punches my arm. "Ok, ok, you got me. I guess you turned out way smarter than me!"

I wait for the laughter to die down. "But for real, how did you know it was me?"

Younger Uncle smiles. "Remember it's a small island. Everyone knows everyone."

"And?"

"The guy at the car rental place is a friend of mine," Younger Uncle says. "He called me to ask if a Yi Kyung-seok was my relative. He said it wasn't the surname. It was because this particular Yi had those," he says pointing first to my dragon and then to my tiger. "Let's be honest. It's not every day two people with the same surname have the exact same tats in the exact same place." He looks into my eyes. "And the same chilling eyes."

27.

Strike delivers the punchline to a joke about excrement, and it triggers
a chorus of guffaws in which Younger Uncle is the loudest. But I'm
quiet. Doesn't seem right for me to be clowning around, not with all the
serious questions whizzing around in my head. I touch my brow, it feels
funny and tingly inside. The strange feeling jumps down and turns into a
quiver in my gut. What is it? Nervous energy?

Maybe a cigarette will help. I light up and smoke while Younger Uncle
and my boys keep going with their merriment. My eyes wander and come
to rest on the only decoration in this bare bones place—an old painting
hanging near the entrance to the kitchen. Five men dressed in traditional
attire are dancing. At the bottom, there's a row of seated women, singing,
I think. I remember a book on ancient Korean culture I'd read in Dad's
den. There was a section on music, how people used to sing to turn their
sorrow into joy. Come to think of it, my boys and I do that in noraebangs
all the time. I smile inside, picturing myself belting out a tune right here,

right now. Since I'm not about to do that, I settle on trying to be optimistic. I mean, the good news is I did find Younger Uncle.

I tilt my chair back and squint as I study this man.

Yi Man-sik. My younger uncle. *A light in the darkness of my life?* I take a drag and turn my head to the side to exhale curly wisps. Yes. *A light in the dark.*

He and my boys are in the thick of their crude humor. The old man stands and helps the old woman up. They shuffle to the door, peeking at Younger Uncle and my boys who are in stitches. When they get to the door, the old man doesn't bother to open the umbrella. It's sunny now.

I check my pocket watch. It's been almost an hour of nonstop good times for Younger Uncle and my boys and they aren't even drinking soju.

This is good. *This is how things should be. Everything is ok.*

The weird sensations are gone. It's only my calm heart beat.

Everything is ok.

Their laughter fizzles out.

Then Strike's eyes sparkle, he ducks his head. Younger Uncle, Braid, and Patch follow suit. Strike touches his cheek and whispers something about a father kissing a mother on the cheek…

His voice fades, but his lips are still moving because I'm suddenly in my head.

Mom touches her cheek and winces. She looks at Older Uncle."You know he's the one that always tells me, 'When trouble comes, it's your family who supports you.'" She moans, then winces again, holding her cheek.

Older Uncle nods. "That's how it's supposed to be. He's forgotten something more important than the code—his family."

How could Dad forget about his family?

Nothing's ok anymore. It feels like every cell in my body drank a pot of coffee followed by a soju chaser. I want to run. I want to hide. But the same old tired questions colliding in my head are ropes that tie me to the chair. *Where's Mom? Why did she leave? How could Dad be so cruel to Mom, me, and basically anyone that doesn't do what he wants? Why did Dad banish Younger Uncle? Why did Older Uncle have to die so young?*

The same old tired hurt whips me, hard.

Boisterous laughter, faraway.

The muffled mix of snickering and rowdy mirth becomes a little louder, a little clearer. It slows to intermittent chuckles.

Younger Uncle says something about a noraebang...

Older Uncle hands Mom a glass of water. "I'm sorry," he says.

"Boss?"

"I'm still your family. I'll help you and Kyung-seok..."

An elbow nudge to my arm. "Boss?" Braid asks.

I blink and look around. "Yes?"

"Let's go check out the noraebang?" Braid suggests.

I turn to Younger Uncle. He nods and says, "You boys go ahead. Come to my house when you're done."

But I don't want to go. I need answers. Isn't that why I'm here? I look at Braid. "Go for it. I'm gonna stay and hang with Younger Uncle."

Braid looks at Strike and Patch. They shrug. Braid looks back at me. "Are you sure we can't convince you?" he asks.

"I'm sure," I say. My boys won't go unless I'm really ok with it. I love them for that. So loyal. And it's not just about this noraebang. They dropped everything to be here with me on this island, didn't they?

"A little singing always makes everything better," Braid coaxes.

I look at the painting and nod. I turn to Braid. "Go on. Have fun. I'll be here with Younger Uncle."

"Okay, boss," he says. "We'll be back in an hour or so."

"Take your time," I say crushing my cig on the bottom of my shoe.

My boys dash faster than Seoul's average internet connection speed, which happens to be the fastest in the world.

Now it's Younger Uncle and me. Face-to-face. Family.

Family is one of nature's masterpieces.

My masterpiece is a disaster. *Mom split. Dad hits. Is Younger Uncle legit?*

Younger Uncle's eyes are on me, soft and accepting.

I rack my brain for any memory of him and me. Nothing at the moment.

"You look exactly like your dad," he says.

"So do you," I say, then sneer. "Aren't you tired of people saying that? I am. I mean I used to think that was so cool, but now—" I cut myself off. Drop my eyes.

"But now—what?"

I touch my right eye. The outer skin is still yellow-tinged, but it isn't sore at all anymore.

Younger Uncle cocks his head to the side, inspecting my healing eye. "I wasn't going to bring it up, but who gave you the shiner? What, ten to fourteen days ago or so?"

I raise an eyebrow. Twelve days ago. Damn.

I pull out my Dunhill tin. I don't bother offering him a cig. He already told me he quit. I light up and take a soothing drag. I exhale a cloud of relief. Then I say, "My dad's handiwork. A memento of life under his grand tutelage. And though I hated him for it, right now I'm glad he did it. It's the reason I'm here. It's the reason I found you."

Younger Uncle smiles, then frowns. His right upper lip and nostril rise in disgust. "Your dad. Figures," he says. "He never stopped punching things," he mumbles, staring at the table.

"What do you mean, he never stopped punching things?"

He lifts his head. "When we were kids, the three of us would be off in some corner of this island, running amok. Dae-sung would always find some poor innocent creature to beat and sometimes kill. One time, Nam-il and I found him hunched over a dead cat, his hand bloody. He had this sinister smile. I started sobbing, but then he punched me in the gut. Nam-il punched him back." He pauses to take a swig of water. "Nam-il would never give him more than what he gave us. So that day it was a punch in the gut for a punch in the gut. But we didn't know how to give an eye for an eye for a dead cat."

I give a slow stroke to my sideburn. *So Dad's always been a cold-blooded killer.* "You know he tortures and kills anyone he considers to be his TSP enemy."

Younger Uncle nods. "It's true. That's one of the reasons I left the gang. Extortion, selling drugs I can sort of live with, but needless killing…" He shakes his head. "That's where I drew a line." He lifts his shirt. His chest is a blank canvas of taut skin over toned muscles with the exception of a few raised pink scars.

"Yeah, I know," he says. "I got all the tats on my chest and back removed when I quit TSP. No three stars on this body." He lets go of his shirt, and it comes down like a stage curtain.

But his show isn't over yet. He pushes up his sleeves. His dragon and tiger posture. "I kept these beasts so I'll never forget how brutal TSP was. Is. And so I'll never forget the things I've done. The things I regret."

"But you left the gang. You're not brutal anymore. Seems to me like you could get rid of those if you wanted."

"I thought about that," he whispers, then sad-smiles. "The thing is, I can't take back the bad things I've done. And there were times I had a chance to stop your dad from killing people. I didn't." He strokes his dragon. Then his tiger. "I keep these as penance, though I know it's not enough…"

I get it. "Were there other reasons you left?" I ask.

He looks at me, pulls his sleeves down. "I'll tell you. But first, you tell me something." He points to my right eye. "How is your shiner the reason you're here?"

"Dad punched me. So I punched the wall in his den. Actually I threw something, and it made a hole in the drywall and this"—I reach into my pocket, bring out the envelope—"this fell to the floor." I put the envelope on the table.

Younger Uncle picks it up, examines it.

"I had so many unanswered questions. I convinced myself that maybe this island had the answers." I take a draw, exhale a smoke stream. "So I told my boys everything, and here we are."

"Glad you're here," Younger Uncle says.

I reach inside my dress shirt and pull out the TSP medallion. "I found this in Dad's den too. It's Older Uncle's, I think." I unclasp the chain, hold the heavy necklace up. The medallion swings like a hypnosis pendant.

Younger Uncle shakes his head. "No, that's mine."

"How do you know?"

He points to the medallion. "One of the diamonds is missing."

I check. Sure enough there's a little empty dip on the right side.

"I sent it back to your dad after I moved here," he says. He fans himself with the envelope. "And I sent him this too."

"What was inside?" I ask.

"I wrote to ask how you were doing. He never wrote back. And actually, I wrote many times to ask about you. I never got a response."

"Oh." I slow stroke my sideburn, looking at the necklace. "Well, I'm guessing you don't want this, right?"

Younger Uncle's eyes narrow as he nods. "No star tats. No star medallion. It's all bullshit."

I shove the chain and medallion into my jacket pocket. "Ok, your turn," I say. "What are the other reasons you left the gang? Dad said he banished you."

He shakes his head. "No. He didn't exactly banish me. It was my choice to leave." His gloomy eyes drop down and he winces.

"Younger Uncle?"

He rubs his eyes, then tries to smile.

"What is it?"

He looks at me with a fixed expression. "I had to leave. See, I was in love with your mother."

My rock face turns into a fish face: gape-mouthed. A first for me.

28.

Mom's last film opened with her in a dingy, dark restaurant, heartbroken and immobile under a wide-brimmed hat. Smoke spiraled from her cigarette. That's Younger Uncle and me now. He's resting his forehead on his palm, like he's overcome with exhaustion, and I'm silently counting every tiny scratch on the table, a rivulet of smoke rising from the Dunhill dangling between my fingers.

It's quiet in the restaurant except for the chop chop chop of vegetables in the kitchen. When it feels right to stop counting, I look up. Soft white light spills in from the many-paned window, it narrows into slivers that cut across our table top. Outside, dark green leaves brush the thin glass, whisking away leftover raindrops. So many leaves within the splintered frame…

Before I know it I'm committed to counting.

But Younger Uncle's hard cough ends that obligation.

I put out my cig and look at him. "Are you ok?"

He nods, even though his face is red and scrunched up and his eyes are watery. He's about to say something, but then he coughs again, takes a sip of water. "All those years smoking," he says before coughing one more time. He guzzles the rest of the water, sets the empty glass down. A second later he shoves it clear across the table.

I catch it just as it goes over the edge.

Younger Uncle looks away, his jaw clenched. Squiggly veins pop out of his temple.

"Are you sure you're ok?"

"I—" he starts but cuts himself off. He takes a deep breath, exhales, and tries again. "I was in love with your mom, but she cared about me like a brother. Nothing more. She was very loyal to your dad. I have to admit I tried a couple of times, but she always refused my advances." He gazes out the window, stroking his upper lip to his chin. In a soft voice he says, "She loved your dad. She was always faithful. But your dad, he did things to her..." He presses his lips together, and his shoulders bow.

"What things?" I ask. I quick make myself imagine her on our balcony with a serene smile, rain bathing her city and opera caressing her soul... because I don't want to know what things.

He shakes his head a little, reaching for his empty glass. He twirls it a few times, then drags his hand back towards his body, slow, like a turtle drawing its head into its shell. He pounds his fist on the table.

I jump a little.

His eyelids are stretched apart as far as they'll go. Tiny ripe, red veins mottle the whites of his eyes. "It made me so mad when he beat her," he growls. "I couldn't take it. Nam-il and I tried to intervene, but your dad wouldn't have it." His face starts glowing like embers. Soon it's as red as the burning tip of my last cig. "'Stay away or I'll kill her,' he said, 'and then you. And what will happen to poor Rocky?' That was the first and only time in my life I wanted to go beyond an eye for an eye. I wanted to kill him. But then I'd be just like him." He massages his temples. His voice is brittle when he says, "I didn't want anything to happen to you or your mother."

An ocean of memories drowns me.

She's crying, holding her cheek.

She's sleeping at noon.

She's crouched in the corner. Stringy hair. Sweaty. Red eyes. Picking, picking, picking. A worn-out baggie of crystals. A pipe…

My fingers twitch. I draw my blade and throw it.

Younger Uncle turns and gapes for a second at the quivering knife sticking out of the wood panel behind him. He faces me again and says, "An expert, I see."

But I'm not thinking about my knife. "Did you know she got into meth?" I hold my breath.

"Yes."

"Why!? Why would she…"

Younger Uncle blows out slowly. "It's complicated," he says.

"No!" I blurt. "What's complicated about that? She was a junkie! She picked drugs over me!"

Younger Uncle reaches over and lays his hand on the sleeve of my jacket. "No," he says. "She wasn't. She didn't. She did what she had to do to take care of you and—"

I don't let him finish. "That's bullshit! I want her to say it to my face. Where is she?"

"She's...she's..."

"Where?!"

He squeezes my arm but doesn't say anything.

"Come on!"

"Rocky, listen. Calm down. I—"

"Calm down?" I kick the table. "How can I—"

"I know. But please try," he whispers. "It's hard for me to talk about this, and your being upset doesn't help."

I blow out my cheeks, then hunch over. "I'm sorry."

He lifts his hand and drapes it on my shoulder. "Your mother...she... she wanted to take you with her."

"Take me with her?" I ask. "Where? When?" I grab a cig, light up, and start smoking the shit out of it.

Younger Uncle sweeps his hand over his face. "Everything happened so fast." He balances his temples on a tripod of fingers and thumbs. "It was bad. Really bad, Rocky. It started way before that night your dad took her to the Han, but that's where it sort of ended," he says.

It sort of ended at the Han? I always end up at the Han.

He spreads his palms on the table and makes small circles. "They got into a fight, and he got physical which wasn't new." His fingers curl in. "But that night at the Han, he thought he'd killed her."

He thought he'd killed her.

Time stops. I'm in a black hole, and it's completely silent.

A voice. Far, far away. "Rocky?"

I hear myself ask, "Wait, he killed her?"

Younger Uncle shakes his head in slow motion, his lips move in slow motion.

I read them.

He thought he'd killed her.

I'm quaking like an earthquake inside, but my body is still. *He thought he'd killed her.* I touch my ears. Younger Uncle's voice comes scraping and grating back, fingernails on a chalkboard.

"But she wasn't dead. She called me…" He taps his knuckles on his lips.

"And then?"

"She wanted to go back to the penthouse right away to get you and leave for good. You were only six at the time. But I told her to stay put." A soft breath escapes from between his lips. "I hated myself for advising her to do that, but if your father found out she was still alive, he would kill her for sure."

My brows bump together, my vision is blurry. "Mom wanted to get me, and you told her not to?"

"Oh, Rocky. Your dad would've killed her. And maybe even you. That's how vengeful he was. Is."

"She-she didn't try again? She didn't try to get me another time?"

"Your mom and I schemed all the time. So many different plans. We tried several times. But your dad had his men on you. Even at school."

Black suits, red pocket squares. In-su and Chul-moo…

"Nothing was working. There was only one option—wait until you were an adult. Until you didn't need your dad's permission to do things. Until you could leave the penthouse for university. He wouldn't stop you from doing that…"

I can't hear him anymore, too many tears.

Younger Uncle holds out his handkerchief.

I shake my head, sucking in my snot. I force myself to stop crying. "I'm ok," I say.

"Your mother loves you more than anything," Younger Uncle says.

Mom loves me more than anything.

My tears return, but slow this time.

I count the fresh ones that end up on my lips.

"She misses you," he says. He puts his hands together in prayer and presses his lips onto the tips of his index fingers.

"How do you know?" I ask.

"She tells me when we talk on the phone."

"What else does she say?"

"She dies a little each day that passes without you. But she will pay that price to keep you safe." Then his eyes and his words implore. "Please understand the seriousness of the situation, Rocky, your dad's brutality has no limits. Your mother had absolutely no choice but to stay away in order to take care of you."

I scrub my face with both hands. *No more tears.* "Where is she?"

"In Los Angeles. I helped her get out of the country within twenty-four hours of her supposed death. That was the only way."

"Is she ok?"

"Yes."

My eyes well up again. I blink hard. *No more tears.*

Younger Uncle half smiles. "You know, she's kept an eye on you—from a safe distance. Far enough to not put either of you in jeopardy. She's flown to Seoul a couple of times a year, every year, since she left."

My face contorts.

"I don't know if you're aware that she's a pretty good photographer. She bought a fancy camera and in different disguises—something she learned in the movies, right?—she's taken lots of photos of you."

My eyebrows shoot up. "Photos of me?"

He nods. "At school. Near the penthouse. At the Han."

My brain starts to close up shop. But it has a grand opening with what Younger Uncle says next.

"She's waiting to show you the album."

29.

The Willow Tree Spa sits high on a hill overlooking Seoul. It's the most expensive and luxurious day spa in all of South Korea: a playground for the rich and famous from here, there, and everywhere. In my dad's case, *his* playground for the rich and *infamous* every Sunday afternoon. I can't believe I thought he kept going because he wanted to keep up the weekly tradition he had with Mom, cherish their good times as a couple, not bask in the selfishness of still being able to go despite 'murdering' her.

Younger Uncle and I drive up the winding road and park near the bottom of some wide stone steps. We come to the entrance—a narrow passageway between two rows of willows, their sweeping branches forming an extended canopy. We breathe in the quiet.

I slide my hands in my pockets. One hugs mom's handkerchief. I trace the stitched willow.

I picture my dad steaming or soaking within these elegant walls. He'll have no excuse to avoid me here. And hopefully he'll be too relaxed to greet me with a fist in the face. *Maybe not.* Because I get it now—there's always a calm before a storm for him. *His* calm before *his* storm.

He thought he'd killed her.

I'm calm outside, but my own storm brews inside. Part of me wants to fight, part of me wants to flee.

I have to fight.

Besides, this isn't bullying. This isn't needless fighting. This is my only way out of a life of perpetual violence.

I have to fight one more time.

Plus Younger Uncle's the ace up my sleeve. Dad has no idea he's in Seoul.

Younger Uncle gives me a chin up. "Ready?"

"Always." My hand settles on my knife.

We enter the passageway, heading for the lobby. The silence screams. It's the kind of movie-scene-quiet right before you get stabbed in the back. And suddenly I'm chilled to the bone.

A spa attendant carrying towels skids to a halt when he sees us. Pivots on his heels, then shrinks into a large closet.

Younger Uncle shrugs.

We keep going. It's so odd that there aren't any other customers sashaying within these posh walls—just how my dad likes it. Yeah, that's right: what my dad wants, my dad gets.

Like everyone in Seoul, the spa owners know that. So without fail they've shut the place down for "a private event" every Sunday afternoon since my parents started coming. I wonder what Mom thought about that.

We take a right into a wide corridor. Though we're treading lightly, the stillness of everything amplifies the sound of our footsteps on the marble floor.

We turn left into a narrower hallway.

Oh shit! Do-hyun and Hak-kun.

My breath gets caught in my chest.

"He's going to have his most trusted men on guard," Younger Uncle says. "We've got to be ready."

I nod. "What do you have in mind?"

Younger Uncle smiles. "Pressure points. It's actually quite an intricate method, you should study it sometime. But for our purposes, I'll teach you a simple combination with proper direction and angle. We'll knock them out but not kill them. That'll give us enough time."

I take a quick look at Younger Uncle. He gives me a *do-what-we-discussed* nod. I clear the static in my brain and rapid review the plan.

"Strike the chin, center of the thorax, and the center of the abdomen," Younger Uncle says, placing a finger on each respective body part. "It's all in the speed, force, and accuracy." Then he raises his fists. "When I say 'a family reunion,' do it like this…"

Younger Uncle starts the show. He grins and waves. "Hello, boys!" he calls out.

Do-hyun and Hak-kun exchange glances, but don't greet us back.

Instead they show force by standing with crossed arms on their pushed-out chests. They stare at us, unblinking.

I thought I was ready to fight, but now I want to flee. I have to force myself to keep walking in their direction.

We reach them. Younger Uncle stands tall in front of Do-hyun. I'm close to Hak-kun.

Younger Uncle holds his hand out for a shake. Do-hyun doesn't reciprocate.

"Well, then," Younger Uncle says, smoothing his hair with the hand Do-hyun left hanging. He looks back and forth between Do-hyun and Hak-kun. "You're not happy to see the youngest star?" he asks as he lowers his hand.

Do-hyun and Hak-kun still don't say anything.

I realize it's the first time I've been in the company of TSP members without my Dad. *I'm playing with the big boys now, Dad.* I smile inside as my apprehension melts into excitement.

Finally Do-hyun opens his mouth. "The boss isn't expecting you," he says in a taut voice. He squints at Younger Uncle.

"Oh, I know," Younger Uncle replies patting Do-hyun on the shoulder. "We wanted to surprise him. A family reunion…"

Younger Uncle and I move in perfect rhythm. Four fists in sync deliver fast jabs to the pressure points.

It's all in the speed, force, and accuracy.

Indeed.

Do-hyun and Hak-kun drop like torn sky dancers.

I'm stuck for a second with my fists up, stunned at the effectiveness of the technique.

Younger Uncle gives me a half smile. "Let's go," he says.

I nod. My hands relax and fall to my side.

We turn left into a room that reminds me of Gyeongbokgung's throne room at the peak of the Joseon dynasty. Rich reds, greens, yellows, and blues burst in traditional designs on the walls, pillars, and ceiling. Shimmery gold cloth chairs, like royal thrones. I picture my dad sitting in one. The tyrannical king of Seoul who thinks he killed the queen. But she's not dead. I guess that makes me the angry prince hellbent on revenge.

I scowl inside.

I don't want that kind of revenge. I don't want to kill the king because I'm not a murderous maniac like him. I want out of the king's bloody reign. I want reunification with the queen in the faraway land she's fled to.

We pass by the outdoor heated pool. The massage and facial rooms. He's not there.

We head to the sauna rooms. Forest room. Jade room. Hot stone room. He's not in any of those.

A biting shiver in my spine comes like on the night when my boys and I were kids and we dared each other to walk alone through a cemetery. The thick air sucks my shallow breath into an invisible graveyard.

We're deep in the guts of the spa now. Ice room. Flower room. No luck.

Get to the salt room. I transform into a guard dog on high alert. I touch my brow, it's slick.

My body feels it—my father's presence.

"He's here," I say.

Younger Uncle nods. Then he puts his hand on my shoulder. "You ok?" he asks.

I lean forward and press my hand on my chest. Nod. Take deeper, slower breaths. Three exactly. Grip my knife.

But then In-su and Chul-moo, black suits with red pocket squares, step out of the shadows.

He had his men on you. Even at school.

Even at the Han. Even here, even there. *Everywhere*? My clammy hand slips off the knife handle.

Younger Uncle clasps his hands behind his body. He saunters up to them, head lifted, chest out. Then he lays his hand on his heart. "It's been awhile," he says, looking at each of them in turn.

In-su draws his gun and holds it in front of his body. Chul-moo does the same with his.

Younger Uncle chuckles. "So it's like that?" He pauses, then adds, "After all we've been through?"

I'm numb. I let Younger Uncle lead the show while I try not to cower in front of these men who've protected my dad and helped him take TSP to the highest of heights.

He had his men keep an eye on me so Mom or Younger Uncle couldn't get to me. They helped my dad keep me away from the truth…

Younger Uncle's talking.

In-su and Chul-moo haven't spoken yet.

Then Younger Uncle examines his fingernails. "Anyway, we're here to surprise my brother. A family—"

A loud creak. The door of the salt room opens, interrupting Younger Uncle's attack phrase. We all look up to see Dad in nothing but his tats and gold chain and medallion.

"I thought I heard a familiar voice," he says, looking straight at Younger Uncle. "It's nice to see you, Man-sik." He quick looks at me, then steps to the side. "Come in, come in," he says waving at us.

We enter the room.

Before Dad closes the heavy wooden door he tells In-su and Chul-moo not to let anyone interrupt his "family time, no matter what."

I scoff inside.

The room is temperature and stylistically cool. Its walls glow pink-orange from the Himalayan salt blocks. Dad sprawls out on a chaise. The three stars on his chest rise as he takes a big breath of the dry salt air. "This is my favorite room," he says. He glances at his gun on the salt floor.

Younger Uncle's looking at it too. "You won't need that," he says. "We're family, right?"

Dad eyes are still on the gun, but now his jaw is clenched.

"Besides," Younger Uncle says, "I've got a friend out there who will email a certain letter to three Seoul police superintendents if I don't call him by seven p.m. with the assurance that Rocky and I are alright." He pauses to smile. "I took my time with it. The letter, that is. I had to make sure I got it right. Didn't want to leave out any of TSP's illegal activities or any of the names of the police on your payroll." He taps his chin. "I wonder what would happen if my friend pressed send…"

Tiny muscles on Dad's flushed face twitch.

"But there's nothing to worry about, is there, Older Brother? No emails need to be sent to anyone, right? We'll just have a little talk, and then Rocky and I will be on our way." He throws a towel on Dad. It lands strategically. "We were close, but not that close," he says, then laughs.

Dad loosens up and laughs too.

Younger Uncle sits in the chair next to Dad. He points to the third chair on the other side of Dad. "Sit," he tells me with a smile.

I do.

Dad grins. Leans forward to slap his younger brother on the back. "It's great to see you. How've you been?"

Younger Uncle goes with it. "Good. Island life is peaceful now that I've learned to ignore the continuous reminders of living on the front line."

Dad nods.

Awkward silence.

Younger Uncle breaks it. "Look," he says to my dad, "Rocky and I have some questions."

"Rocky AND you?" Dad asks in a sarcastic voice. He smirks as he laces his fingers behind his head. His tats pop on the flexed muscles of his arms and chest. "Questions? About what?" He holds up his finger. "Wait. Let me guess. You want back in TSP? And Rocky wants in. That's it, isn't it?" He wags his finger at me. "You're a smart one, dragging your uncle all the way here to get your way. I told you we'll see about all that after you finish university. Anyway you know your mother would say no." He gives Younger Uncle a sly glance. "Although she might not say no to your younger uncle here."

Younger Uncle ignores Dad's insinuation. "I'll get right to it. Was Bo-young using meth?" he asks brushing some lint off the sleeve of his suit jacket.

"Why do you want to know?" Dad asks with a slight head tilt.

Younger Uncle squares his leg over his knee and leans forward. "Because I think Rocky deserves to know the truth about his mother."

"Stop right there," Dad says putting his palms up. "Rocky's my son. I think I know what's best for him."

That's the funniest and saddest thing my dad's ever said. My insides don't know whether to laugh or cry. Both?

"What a shame if that email goes out…" Younger Uncle shrugs.

Dad huffs, then mumbles, "She was using."

My body stiffens.

"Why?" Younger Uncle asks.

Dad circles a shoulder. "You really want to know?" he asks, his tone biting.

Younger Uncle nods.

"Because of you!" Dad shouts.

Younger Uncle draws back. "Me? What?"

I applaud Younger Uncle's theatrical skills in my head.

Dad looks at me. "Did you know your younger uncle over here was having an affair with your mother?" There's desperation in his voice. "Did you know that, Rocky?"

I don't respond.

Dad sits back and looks at Younger Uncle. His eyebrows form a V. "What is this? What's really going on?"

"Tell us why Bo-young started using," Younger Uncle demands.

Dad's face turns lava red. "Because she was weak," he snarls.

"No, she wasn't!" I blurt, but then I seal my lips because I'm not supposed to say anything yet. That's not part of our plan.

Younger Uncle isn't thrown off a bit. "Weak?" he asks. "You mean she couldn't resist partying or something?"

Dad snickers. "Bo-young certainly liked to party, but that wasn't it. She never would've gotten into the stuff on her own. That was all me. She was in one of her lows, and I had some G.I. contacts slip her the crystal. I had a feeling she'd try it because she was drinking more anyway and talking about how her life was 'nothing but getting through Dae-sung's hell on earth.' I'll give her credit, though, because she loved the first crystal high, 'the flash' as she called it, but she didn't want to keep using—see I had the G.I.s keep giving her the stuff. She asked me to get them to stop. Consider it done, I told her." He smiles all wicked. "But, one night I brought some of it home. Maybe we can get high together, honey? I only watched her use, I never touched the stuff myself. TSP code, right? Anyway, the rest is history, I was her husband and dealer." His face changes. "She deserved everything she got," he mutters under his breath. "She..."

But I'm done listening to him because I'm listening to the orders my head is shouting. *Lunge! Choke him!* I tell my head to shut up and stick to the plan. *Dad has to believe we think he killed Mom—which he pretty much did, killed her from my life anyway—so that when I move out he won't bother me ever again. He'll get that I don't want anything to do with him since he murdered my mom. Even a psycho killer can understand that. And respect it.*

I force myself to transform into a true thespian in an improv theater because I'm up. I follow Dad's lead but know that my goal is to steer him to admit everything. "So you got her hooked," I say with fake confusion in my voice and a perfect frown on my face. I'm betting that Dad's arrogance won't let him not keep going with the "truth" as he sees it.

And I'm right.

Dad keeps his eyes fixed on Younger Uncle when he says, "A woman like that—so beautiful, so many men wanting her—has to be put in her place now and then with a slap or a punch. But if she starts sneaking around, it takes more extreme measures to keep her in line. Especially when she's sneaking off with your younger brother—"

Younger Uncle interrupts. "That's not true, you know—"

Dad interrupts back. "And so I had to beat her lying, adulterous ass harder, and more often. I had to keep her strung out to keep her away from you. Revenge never felt so good as when I saw her crashing off the stuff…all alone…a complete mess." He brandishes his fist. "How dare she cheat on me! How dare you try to steal her away from me!"

He turns to me, and his eyes douse me in his hate. "A couple of times she tried to take you and leave me. I promised that if she ever tried to leave again—or even spoke about leaving—I'd kill her." He looks away, his eyes soften for a second, glisten even, but then he rubs them and scowls. "And maybe her beloved Rocky, too."

My fingers wrap around my knife. I'm this close to pulling it out, I'm not acting anymore.

Dad's eyes don't hesitate, they throw daggers at Younger Uncle. "It's a good thing you decided to leave Seoul when you did," Dad says. He smiles a creepy half smile. "She was so, so weak," he says.

I break. My knife's out, and I'm standing over Dad. "She wasn't weak! She wasn't! She—"

Dad jumps up and gets in my face. "Do it, Rocky," he dares. "Come on! Let me see what you're made of," he roars.

I don't move. I stand there, clutching my knife next to my head, sweating like we're in the hottest sauna room.

My dad smiles. "Yeah, that's what I thought. You're weak. Just like your mother. Sit your ass down," he commands.

Younger Uncle's voice is gentle as he goes off script. "It's ok, Rocky, please put the knife away. Please sit down."

I do what he says.

Dad lowers himself down too.

"Listen, Dae-sung, we know she didn't leave. We know you killed her. Why?" Younger Uncle asks, sticking to our rehearsed lines.

Dad doesn't respond. He clenches his forearms with his opposite hands and digs into his own flesh.

Younger Uncle asks again.

"I…I…" Dad begins but can't finish. His curled upper lip quivers.

Suddenly he pounces on Younger Uncle, fists flying. Before I have a chance to do anything, Younger Uncle gets Dad into a stranglehold. Dad writhes and slaps one palm on Younger Uncle's arm and the other on the chair. Younger Uncle loosens his hold just enough that Dad can get some air but can't do anything else.

I'm poised over Dad again, this time my fists are up.

Younger Uncle keeps one arm around Dad's neck and motions for me to sit with his free hand.

I do.

Then Younger Uncle chokes dad. "You calm?" he asks. He releases the pressure a little so Dad can answer.

"Yes," Dad says, frowning.

Younger Uncle lets go.

Dad clutches his neck, breathing hard.

Younger Uncles asks again. "Why did you kill her?"

Dad finishes catching his breath. "I kept my promise. She insisted she was leaving with Rocky, and that this time nothing would stop her." Then he stares into space and touches his neck. "So I stopped her," he says in a robotic voice. "There was terror in her eyes as I squeezed." He holds his hands up, flips them to inspect the front and back. His lips curve up into a menacing smile. Then he fixes Younger Uncle in a stare that could freeze the Yellow Sea. "How did you know?"

"You're not the only one good at digging up dirt," Younger Uncle says.

My dad looks past Younger Uncle. "If only you two had stayed away from each other, then none of this would've happened," he mumbles. He cranks his gaze back to Younger Uncle and yells, "Then she wouldn't be dead!"

Dad keeps talking. But I can't hear him. All I hear is my mom's voice.

"*I love you more than anything.*"

"*Mom! Mom!*"

Ghost hands slide over my ears, mouth, and nose. Clamp down. My heart goes into overdrive, beating wildly. Another ghost squeezes my ribs with its invisible lead arms. I can't breathe. Younger Uncle's lips move on his worried face.

Everything is far away. Everything gets fuzzy. Goes gray. Dark. Darker...

30.

On this cool, windy evening, the soles of my Oxfords smack all the cracks, not to mention all the splotches of gum and dead leaves. I keep tripping on sidewalk bumps. My heart thuds and spasms in an erratic rhythm. I cram my hands in my pockets and hunch over. I count the restaurants on this block, then lose count. I try the trees instead. *One, two, three, four, four, four...*Get stuck on four. My heart freaks out, my breath gets shallow. The sweat on my brow and in my pits broadcasts my fear.

I tap, I trace, but the city I've walked my entire life has turned its back on me. And then it closes in, angry. The skyscrapers, the cars, the street lamps, the signs—they chase me. My feet lift higher, faster, and soon I'm not walking at all. My pumping arms and rhythmic breathing in hot spurts match my long strides.

I slip on a slick patch—the only remaining evidence of the earlier downpour—as I round a corner. There's a low growling behind me, and I quick look over my shoulder. Seoul's sharp claws reach out...

I keep running.

Until I'm not. I look down. My right foot is on a boardwalk and straight ahead, the Mapo Bridge. Seoul slinks away as if I've thrown it off my track. Maybe I've disappeared into another dimension.

I walk, a little more steady. My heart slows, my breath eases, and the sweat dries up. I scan the Yeongdeungpo side in the distance. The highest dusk sky is purple, it blends gradually into blue, light blue, tangerine, and red-orange. The clouds are thin, frayed tufts emerging from the cityscape. The highrise lights sprinkle bright dots on the silky black Han.

Lights, so many lights. So many people awake. Seoul never sleeps.

Cars speed by.

So many people...

But I'm alone.

There are government-issued signs with quotes at regular intervals on the handrails.

How are you doing?

Have you been eating alright?

Isn't it nice walking on a bridge?

My gut twists, and I shout answers in mind.

Shitty!

No!

Hell no!

I remember the girl, Woo-jin's victim, who killed herself here. She must've read these lame questions. Did she have the same answers as me? Did she feel alone, forsaken, like me? Is that why she jumped?

I want to pound all these signs.

I pass by some government-issued photos of happy babies and kids and families alongside the quotes.

I go slack for a second, then everything slumps. My shoulders. My eyes. My thoughts.

There's a bench up ahead. I could use a rest.

Part of the bench is already occupied by a bronze statue of two people. *How come I've never noticed it before?* I get closer. The boardwalk creaks under my cautious steps. I'm in front of it now. A glum teen boy slouches, staring at the nothingness that is his life. A smiling older man, maybe his dad or grandfather, has one hand on the boy's back, and the other hand is pinching the boy's cheek.

The boy's hands dangle between his knees.

My hands hang limp by my side.

I turn away, keep walking.

A young couple, arm-in-arm, passes by, laughing. The girl puts her head on the guy's shoulder.

Then a family of four approaches. "Happy birthday, son," the dad says. The mom rubs her son's back and the little sister cheers.

More people come and go, but I'm alone. And lonely. I can't brush it off, I stare at the pavement. I don't want to see any more faces. Feet, on the other hand, are ok. They aren't in love or cheerful or proud, they just do their job. Though mine are more unsure tonight.

I stop at the railing, excited voices behind me. My hands drape over the railing and I lean… on it…over it. The hypnotic Han beckons me.

Rocky…

I lean over a little more...

"Rocky!"

My head cogwheels. It's Ha-na standing under a street lamp. Her beautiful eyes are wide and shiny under the bill of a camo print baseball cap with a Korean flag patch. I instantly picture her as a ROK marine. It almost makes me smile.

She crosses her arms, and the sleeves of her jean jacket pull up a little at the wrist giving me a glimpse of her scars.

She looks down and sees what I see so she drops her arms and clasps her hands behind her back.

Without a word I look back at the inviting Han.

Her footsteps.

One, two, three.

Sidelong glance.

She's reaching for my shoulder. "Rocky?" she whispers.

"What?" I snap.

Her hand retreats. "Did you eat yet?" she asks.

Have you been eating alright? Did she read the sign? I don't look at her, only shake my head.

"I'm meeting my parents for some dinner. Do you want to join us or something?" she asks.

I shake my head. *Please go away.*

She comes closer. "Are you sure?" she asks.

"I'm sure!" I roar, then regret, but can't muster the energy or will to retract.

She backs away. "Ok, ok," she says, her voice brittle. She starts to walk away, but then she stops and looks over her shoulder. "Please take care," she mumbles.

Her footsteps fade. I watch the big Indian flag printed on the back of her jacket get smaller and smaller. It disappears. She disappears.

I want to disappear.

Time drifts by like the black river with its twinkling surface.

I realize I'm still here. But if I hoist myself onto this flat part of the railing—

Rocky...

It's Mom's voice this time.

Rocky, don't give up. We'll be together soon.

I let go of the railing and step back. Sorrow punches through my chest, I press one hand on it and sob.

"Boss!"

"Hey, boss!"

I stop crying and pull out my handkerchief to quickly wipe my face. I suck in my snot as I look. Braid, Strike, and Patch are running towards me, waving. Soon they're standing in a semicircle behind me.

"How did you know I was here?" I whisper.

Braid coughs. "Ha-na called," he says. "She was stressing about you."

All those prank calls, and she returns the favor with a call of concern. I'm the lowest of the low.

He steps next to me and looks at my face. "So... what's up, boss?"

I frown and turn my head further away, but Strike and Patch are standing on the other side of me. I have no choice but to look straight ahead at the Han.

"We were gonna go grab some food. Wanna come, boss?" Strike suggests.

Again with eating?

My fists clench, but I don't say anything.

They don't say anything else either.

We all gaze at the Han for awhile. And then awhile longer.

Finally my mouth decides to give up the silent treatment. It opens, and the words convulse out. "I need to—get—out of—this—city."

My boys listen with their eyes.

"My mom, she... " I can't finish because my eyes threaten to unleash again. I blink fast and hard. I want to tell them everything, but I'm all choked up. I close my eyes. My life flashes, everything old, everything new. It passes through me like a category five hurricane. The powerful winds and waves leave me in ruins.

I rip my eyes open. My hand is on my chest, my heart is barely beating underneath. The muscles on my chin tremble as fresh tears spill down my face, a few onto my lips. I lick the salty pain.

Braid edges closer. "She what?" he asks, his voice gentle.

Strike rests his elbow on the railing and his chin on his palm. "Boss?"

"She's..." I start, then seal my lips.

My boys wait.

"She's a refugee," I manage to whisper. *In L.A., instead of here with me.* "My dad thinks he killed her."

Two sharp inhales on either side of me and one forehead smack.

I glance to the right, then left.

Braid's got this piercing stare. Strike's forehead is on the railing. Patch is shaking his head, one hand on his brow.

"You can't tell anyone. Her life, my life, depends on it," I say. "Swear it," I demand. "On your life."

They look at me but don't say anything. Their huge, dark eyes speak of understanding. And though I've always known their loyalty is unwavering, I've never shared a secret this big.

I become a rock, a shouting rock. "Swear it on your life!"

Braid pulls out his pocket knife and slices his palm. A red line dribbles. Strike pulls out his knife, a second slice, a second red line. Then Patch. A third.

Braid holds up his bleeding palm, motions to Strike and Patch to do the same. "On our honor, on our blood, on our life, we swear it," he recites like a sacred oath.

Strike nods. "We swear it."

Patch nods.

Bloody allegiance.

I'm touched, but I remain stone-cold. All I do is give them one hard nod before I turn back to the river and slam my fist on the railing. "Fuck Three Star Pa. Fuck being boss. Fuck my dad. Fuck meth. Fuck money. Fuck this city," I bellow.

"Bo—," Braid starts, then stops. "Rocky," he says instead, "I'm sorry, man." He looks at Strike and Patch.

They nod.

"We're sorry," Strike says. "It's so fucked up."

Braid slides closer. "We got your back, man. No matter what."

"No doubt," Strike says.

Patch nods and thumps his chest.

I look at my boys, at their worried expressions and their sliced hands. *Why are they still standing beside me? How can they still give a shit about me?*

Braid puts his good hand on my shoulder. "You ok?" he asks. His forehead is puckered, and his lips are a thin line.

Strike steps closer and lays his good hand on my other shoulder. "Yeah, Rocky," he says. "You ok?"

Patch pats my back. I look over my shoulder. He tucks his chin and lifts his eyebrows.

I shake my head. "Not really," I whisper.

They don't say anything else, but they keep their hands on me. For a long time we stand like that, staring at the world in front of us. The city. The river. The night sky.

The night sky is full of sparkling stars. Three in particular are especially bright.

My three boys. My three bright stars leading me out of the darkness of Three Star Pa. My boys, more like my brothers.

I'm not alone, and in this moment, I'm not lonely. I'm safe with my bros. My family.

Family is one of nature's masterpieces.

But I'm a piece of sh…

No.

A plain blue sky, even if it's the most gorgeous azure or cerulean, is boring. A silvery cloud or two makes the perfect sky more like real life—imperfect.

I dare to smile ever so slightly inside. *You're right, Mom.*

I've done stupid, cruel, and shitty things, but I'm not a piece of shit. What I am is imperfect. And what I can do is try to make things right, that's what Younger Uncle tries to do every day.

I fish for the gold chain and medallion in my pocket. I bring it out and trace the three glinting stars. Then I crumple it all together and grip the thick wad like it's a baseball and I'm a pitcher. I extend my arm behind me, count to three in my head, then hurl the boss necklace at the batter—the Han. The river misses, and the necklace sinks into the depths.

31.

It's the kind of summer morning when the breeze sleeps in. The grass doesn't bend, the rose bushes don't sway. I pass by a flourishing acacia tree, a thrush is perched on a low branch, singing. The leaves dangle stiff like they're sculpted. The stuffy stillness permeates into my core, makes me stop. I wait in vain for a light wind's embrace. *No luck*. Hands in my pockets, a comfortable slouch, I amble away on the walking path.

Only a few people are out. Up ahead, the two sections of the World Peace Gate's enormous roof remind me of wings. Wings on a giant bird taking flight into the majestic blue sky. I stretch my arms out, pretending they're my wings. I close my eyes and drop my head back a little. Maybe I can soar with this great bird of peace.

When I open my eyes, I'm at the Gate's main entrance. I check my pocket watch, plenty of time until my bros get here. I look up, and my eyes land smack on Ha-na. I cringe.

Damn it. Seriously?

She's cruising under the roof, sketchbook in hand. Her head is tilted back, and the long swell of her hair reminds me of midnight waves. Her eyes are glued to one of the gigantic animal paintings on the ceiling.

She smiles to herself as she whisks her pencil off her ear and gets to work outlining. Soon she's shading. Her smile fades, and her eyebrows furrow. More lines and shading. The tip of her tongue pokes out of the side of her mouth.

I've never seen her with her sketchbook at school, but out in the world it seems to be her third arm.

Her hand transcribes the world onto paper in an elegant waltz... Ha-na the artist doing her thing. I can't help but smile inside as I imagine what her eyes capture—colors and shapes in exquisite detail, beauty in everything with no judgement. Everything equal. Everything indispensable.

She pauses, twirls her hair around her pencil.

Now it's Ha-na the girl. Not a black coolie. Not a beast. Not ugly. Not fat. A girl. A human.

A human who helped me like a guardian angel.

I want to make things right. But if she's not having my sorry, why would she let me make things right? Maybe I should just leave her alone, let her get on with her life in peace.

I pivot on my heels and prepare to make my getaway. But my past cruelty binds my feet and demands to be reviewed, demands reparations for what I've done. Then it grabs my chin and yanks my face in her direction, makes me look at her.

Should I try to make things right? Of course I should! No, I shouldn't. Yes, I should! No. Yes.

I stand there, literally stuck in indecision. It's like someone poured cement that dried in an instant. All I can do is go for a cigarette. I light up and frantic smoke. One last puff before I toss the butt.

Ha-na's eyes dart from the ceiling to her sketchbook. Her pencil is going and going with a determination that impresses me but also make me a little sad because for a second her hand and pencil are like my feet on the streets of Seoul. They have to move. They have to go.

Our survival depends on it.

But we're both safe from our respective demons now. Only I'm not sure if she knows she's safe. I'm not sure if she knows that I will never hurt her, or anyone, again. Not on purpose, at least.

My head spins.

I should give it another go. I should try to make things right.

Younger Uncle would. So I try to lift a foot, this time it budges a little. I drag myself towards her like I'm wading through thick sludge.

When I'm finally standing in front of her, I pull my shoulders back and open my mouth. "Ha-na," I say, "Can I talk to you?"

She ignores me as she looks back and forth between the red phoenix and her sketchbook, shading.

I reach out, slowly. "Ha-na?"

She steps away just as my hand is about to touch her shoulder.

I follow her, I reach out again and give her shoulder a gentle tap.

She doesn't look at me. She doesn't say anything. She keeps on drawing.

I stare at my feet. "I can't believe you helped me. I-I didn't, don't, deserve it," I stammer, shaking my head. I peek at her.

She's engrossed in her work like I'm not even there.

"I'm sorry," I whisper. I rub the back of my neck. I don't know what else to say or do to make things better for her. I check out her drawing. I point to it and say, "Your phoenix is more beautiful than the one on the ceiling." And I mean it.

That's when Ha-na stops drawing. She looks at me with a fixed expression. "You helped me once. I helped you once. Let's call it even. You don't have to talk to me now. You don't have to be nice." She takes three steps away and goes back to shading.

"Wait, I-I..." I start. My head feels like the mayhem at primary school recess. I go to her and try again. "We're not even. I know I can't make up for all the—"

She cuts me off with a groan and an eye roll. She thrusts her sketchbook and pencil at me. "Hold," she demands.

I do.

She pushes her sleeves up to her elbows. Her gruesome scars clamour for me to leave her alone. "One cut for every single time you or anyone has been cruel," she says. She pulls her sleeves down.

I hang my head. "I'm so sorry," I mumble.

She grabs her sketchbook and pencil from me. "I know you think you're sorry."

I look up. *I am sorry.* But I can't get myself to say it again because her words are like a shrink ray, and I feel myself getting smaller and smaller.

Her eyes become glazed with tears. She looks away and turns her back on me to resume her drawing.

I count the cracks on the concrete tiles. But then it's hard to count because everything's blurry. *Fuck*!

32.

I sweep my finger over the dusty cover of the Onkyo, and it leaves a clear, straight path. *That's how long I haven't played my beloved opera.* I release the breath I didn't realize I was holding. *That's how much things have changed.* I wipe the hard plastic cover with a fuzzy cloth, three times, before I carefully lift it to lay the vinyl on the turntable. The stylus next, it bumps up and down on the rotating disc. The crackling sound...I love it.

I step onto the balcony, and the cool air wakes me up like a splash of cold water. A second later Pavarotti's voice announces the dawn. I watch the sun, a ripe glowing persimmon, rise in the blue gray horizon.

I yawn big, my tight facial muscles pump my lacrimal glands, making my eyes water reflexively. I rub the involuntary tears away.

Pavarotti sings sadness.

Now different tears form and escape, melancholic ones. I brush them off my cheek too, but not before Mom's in my head.

Oh, if Pavarotti knew his voice is the only thing that can move my little Rocky.

Another couple of mournful tears.

Not the only thing, Mom.

I look back at the empty black cushion on the acacia wood loveseat. *You should be sitting there. Like you used to with your arms open, waiting for me.*

I rest my hands on the railing, a flood of bittersweet in my head.

Mom the angel. Dad my hero. Opera. Makgeolli. Rain. Dunhills. Laughter.

How could I have known that the *us* on this balcony back then was a lie?

The front door slams, I check my pocket watch.

Speak of the devil. He arrives at 6:11.

I touch my knife handle, trace my stars, my name. The second to the last time.

I slide my hands into my pockets and go inside. Will Dad talk to me today? He's been ignoring me since the spa.

"Good morning, Dad," I say with a bow.

He walks past me. "Good morning," he says, slurring a little.

I follow him. "Can I talk to you?"

He shrugs as he goes to the kitchen and fixes himself a glass of water.

I stand on the other side of the counter and draw my knife. *It gleams like a dream.* That's because I just buffed it an hour ago. I trace my stars, my name. The last time, ever. *Ever.* I put the knife on the counter, push it towards him.

Dad doesn't seem to notice my monumental gesture. He's busy reading the newspaper.

"Dad."

"Huh."

"I'm grateful for this knife, but I don't need it anymore."

He doesn't say anything. He takes a sip of water, keeping his head in the paper.

I try again. "I'm out of the school gang. And no TSP for me. You're right about university. Oh, and I got accepted to one abroad, full scholarship." I thought the TSP and university lines would grab his attention. They don't. I thought he'd ask me where I got in. And for proof. He doesn't.

I uncross my fingers since I don't need to tell the second lie about going to London.

I stare at him, wondering if he's really reading or if he's just ignoring me, or both.

"I don't need to fight anymore, Dad," I say. "Maybe this can be your spare knife?"

"Maybe," he says without looking up.

"Well, ok, then," I say. "I'll be leaving for Baengnyeong tomorrow morning. You know I can't stay with you...not after what you did to Mom." Tears pool. Quick eye rub. I can't believe I couldn't say "since you killed Mom" like I'd practiced. It's horrible even to imagine, and it seems I can't even say the words. But not saying the words minimizes his brutality. I massage my temples because my brain hurts. I decide to abort that part of the mission and skip to the end, "Gonna live with Younger Uncle before leaving Seoul. He said he's already spoken to you about it?"

Younger Uncle and I decided that it would be safer to live with him on the island for a bit before going to "university." That way, Dad wouldn't suspect anything.

Dad lifts his head and folds the newspaper nice and neat, glaring at me. "Why yes, he has spoken to me about that," he says in a hostile voice. He flings the newspaper, it goes flying across the room. He glances at the knife. "How dare you? You selfish, thankless little shit!" He punches the counter. "How dare you and your younger uncle conspire against me."

Automatically, I cower and take a step back.

"You're just like your mother, aren't you?"

My head jerks up, and I jut my chin. "Better her than you," I mutter under my breath.

He charges around the counter and comes at me. "What did you say?"

I hold his stare. "Better her than you."

He pokes his finger in my chest. Screams, "How dare you! How dare—"

I interrupt his self-righteous speech with my own. I manage to cage my fear because, hey, I'm leaving anyway. "Dad, you're the biggest bully. I mean you take bullying to another level. Friends, family, foe, anyone. Not only that, you're a killer! You killed Mom! If I stay here with you, I might turn into you." I step closer to him, disgust makes my body tremble.

He doesn't say a word.

I shake my head, then in my best stone-cold voice I say, "I don't want to be anything like you." I stand straighter and cross my arms. I smile inside because I realize I'm a little taller than him. "I'm outta here."

"How dare you," he says. He shoves me, then goes to punch me, but I grab his fist and twist his arm. He cries out. I twist a little more until he sinks to the ground. Before I know it, my knife isn't on the counter, it's at home in my hand, and I've got it pressed up against my dad's neck. I squeeze the handle. My hand shakes. Sweat beads up on my forehead. A few drops fall on the hardwood floor.

"Do it, Rocky!" he shouts, spraying me with his spit.

I push the blade's sharp edge into his skin and it makes a thin slice into his epidermis and dermis. Bright red line.

"Do it!"

Sweat and tears blind me. I blink fast and hard.

"Do it! What are you waiting for?"

I shake my head. "No," I whisper. "I'm not like you." I let go of the knife, and it lands with a clunk. I release his fist. I back away slowly.

He wipes the blood off his neck, looks at it with curious eyes. Then he tastes it. He looks back at me, glowering with the wildest eyes I've ever seen.

I turn around and head back to my room to pack.

He doesn't follow.

33.

I stare at the nickel-silver keys in my hand. Two keys on the ring—my house key and my car key. I lay them on the console table as I sling my duffel bag over my shoulder. I step out of the penthouse into the quiet, low-lit hallway. I take one more look back inside, back at my life so far, then I lock the door from the inside and pull it shut behind me. I twist the knob to make sure it's locked.

It is.

Locked for the first time.

I start to walk, then pivot on my heels and go back to the door. I turn the knob. It's still locked. I head out again. Stop again, go back to the door again. Check the knob. Of course, it's still locked. I do an about-face and stride to the elevator, relieved that this time I make it.

I arrive in the lobby and leave my bag with the doorman.

Time to walk the streets of Seoul.

One last time.

But I won't be alone.

34.

Dusk slips in. Seoul is teeming with people and cars. But we walk as if it's only us. Braid. Patch. Strike. Me. Me and my boys, me and my brothers, side by side. Our footsteps echo because it's only us. We don't talk. Hand in our pockets, a little slouched: ex-mini gangsters trying to be good citizens.

We're all in sync. And, we don't step on cracks because we really don't want to break anyone's back.

We walk into Seoul's belly. Soon the natural light drains, but the city plugs in and flickers in technicolor. It burns bright in neon yellows, greens, reds, blues, and purples.

People hustle, stroll, and wander, but we walk. We pass by huge department stores, coffee shops, bars, and small restaurants that send forth the delicious scents of garlic and gimchi. There are fruit stands overflowing with giant grapes and ripe figs and street stalls selling knick knacks, watches, and cell phone cases.

But we don't stop. No jobs tonight. No more jobs for me. Ever.

A fine mist covers my face. I look up, and drizzle mixed with a couple of thick drops splatters on my forehead, trickling into my eyes. The rain picks up until there's a steady pitter patter on the streets and the sidewalks. Plinking on cars and signs. Umbrellas everywhere. Except over us. I count the red ones, stop when I get to seven. Lucky seven.

I look down, taking care to avoid the tiny puddles.

The rain stops. Umbrellas, lowered and folded, fall away like domino lines.

We pass by an alley and glance sideways. Five thugs lurk in the shadows. They step forward. I immediately recognize their tacky pinstripe suits. *Woo-jin's mini SGP gang.* Only he's not with them. Still in juvie, I guess. His boys flex. Challenge us with hard, menacing looks.

I don't flinch. My boys don't flinch.

I ignore them. My boys ignore them.

We walk and walk and walk. Until our next step would be into the Han. It stretches before us, like a long arm waiting to wrap around us.

We squat at the water's edge and light up. We smoke, staring at the gentle ripples glinting in the moonlight and city lights.

I rest my arms on my knees and let my cig dangle from my fingers. "You know how to get to the island," I say keeping my eyes on the river.

Braid takes a draw, exhales. "Sure do."

Strike looks at Patch. "Remind me, no donuts on the ferry."

Patch nods.

I reach into my jacket's flap pocket and pull out a square envelope sealed with red wax. I hand it to Braid. "Please give this to Ha-na," I say.

He nods, takes it, and slips it into his inner pocket.

"What is it?" Strike asks.

Patch slaps the back of his head.

"Ouch!" Strike cries. "What?" He rubs his head. "I'm just asking."

"It's ok," I tell Patch then look at Strike. "My apology letter," I say.

"Oh," is all Strike says before giving me a half smile.

I take a long drag. "No more bullying, anyone. And help Ha-na if she needs it," I say even though we've all agreed on this already.

"Of course, bo—," Braid starts but then chuckles and shakes his head. "I mean, Rocky."

Patch and Strike nod.

The Han is barely moving. I close my eyes, imagine...

Mom's sitting on the water's edge. She picks up the bag of crystal and the pipe, her hands trembling. Tears spill down her cheeks, her makeup bleeds. Suddenly she looks up. "Rocky," she says. "I didn't see you there." She drops her eyes and shakes her head. "I'm sorry. I didn't want to leave you."

I walk over, sit next to her.

She drapes her arm on my shoulders. "I love you more than anything, my sweet boy," she whispers, then kisses my forehead. "I'm so sorry," she says. She takes a second to dump the crystal in the Han, then hands me the baggie and pipe. "Toss these in the trash can over there, will you?" she asks, pointing.

I jump up and do it. Then I sit back down next to her. She's still crying softly. I wipe her tears with my handkerchief.

"My willow tree," she says. She smiles. "I was going to make one for you next. For when you grew into a young man."

"I am a young man, Mom."

She leans back to look me up and down. "So you are. And such a handsome one." She holds my face in her hands. "I love you more than anything, young man," she says.

"I know, Mom. I love you, too."

"Do you forgive me?"

I nod.

"Will you come to see me soon?"

The river sloshes against the bank.

I open my eyes. My hand is on my chest and my heart beats calmly inside. Maybe my mom's always been in here.

She strokes my cheek. "Will you?"

"Yes," I reply.

I look at my boys, press my hand a little harder. My boys, my brothers, are in here too.

"Hey," I say to them. "I've got another secret."

They turn to me, move closer.

"The island isn't my final destination."

Wonder pulls apart their eyelids.

I look over my shoulders. All clear. I lean in and whisper my truth. All of it.

Dear Ha-na,

You said "I know you think you're sorry."
But I'm sorry isn't enough. I know that now
For the first time. I see you. Really see you.
Ha-na the artist. Ha-Na the big hearted
human who saved me on the bridge.
I can only hope that one day I might
know you better.

Now I want to hear you, listen to you.
What can I do to make things right
for you? If and when you're ready
to tell me. I'll meet you anywhere
you want. Anywhere, anytime.

Rocky

36.

I'm walking in a field of bright yellow flowers. It's a floral jungle, so different from the concrete one I'm used to. I stop for a second to cradle a flower. This flower breathes too, in its own way—without lungs and without a bloodstream. I rub a leaf just under it, in awe that the little green oval can do that plus turn what I breathe out into oxygen.

A breeze skims along the flowers. They rustle cordially, letting me eavesdrop on their musings. I put my hands out wide in front of me, my fingers grazing the delicate petals. I close my eyes. Far away, Pavarotti sings the highest tenor notes. His voice trickles down from the sky like a sweet rain.

I open my eyes. There are five clouds in the bold blue sky. *Perfectly imperfect.*

My destination is the only willow tree on Baengnyeong. I found it last week when Younger Uncle and I were driving back from Kongdol Beach. We'd spent some hours wading on large submerged rocks, fishing. We caught enough for a hearty dinner. Halfway home we passed by this sea of yellow (on the island that's in the Yellow Sea!). All I saw was the green of rounded, drooping branches that I wanted to come back to.

When I reach the willow, I lean my back against its trunk. Its bark, like a tight bundle of thick ropes, massages me. It's a safe place, a refuge. I sit beneath it and pull out my Dunhill tin. It creaks the same as always when I open it. My parent's wedding photo greets me the same as always. I pluck out a cig, light up, and take slow draws. I give myself plenty of time to enjoy my smoke. It's going to be my last one, ever.

When I'm done, I crush the burning end on the ground and stick the butt in my pocket. There are twenty-three cigarettes left in the tin. I grab a sharp spade from my back pocket and dig a small hole at the base of the willow, piling the damp dirt neatly. I take a deep breath of the fresh soil smell. It cleanses the smokey residue from my lungs. I place my Dunhill tin—my mom's Dunhill tin—in the hole. I smile inside. Then I fill the hole.

Younger Uncle suggested I call Mom. But I thought, what's another week? I've waited this long. Talking to Mom over the phone doesn't seem right.

But I can talk to her here.

I pat the soil mound until it's flat. I dust my hands on my shorts before I press them together in prayer, my head bowed. "Mom, how are you? I'm good. It's been great living with Younger Uncle. He's awesome. He's made this simple life for himself on this beautiful island, and I like it. I think you'd like it, too." I take out my handkerchief, hold it over my head, and trace the stitched willow. "I keep this with me always. It's how I keep you close." I press the handkerchief to my chest, to my heart. Then I put it back in my pocket.

"Guess what, Mom? I'm not fighting anymore. I feel pretty good these days. It's kind of strange." I exhale a long, slow breath before I continue. "I heard a Christian minister at the gas station the other day. He was talking to one of his parishioners, he quoted a verse from the the Bible. 'Then you will know the truth and the truth will set you free.' Well, I'm not Christian or anything, but I think the truth about you and Dad has set me free. I know you didn't want to leave me. I know you really loved me. Love me." I pause to rub my eyes. "I love you too. I promise no more fighting. No more being mean. I will make you proud. I don't know if I'll be a surgeon...maybe...but whatever I do, I will make you proud." I smile. "Dad doesn't like that I'm here, but I don't care. Maybe someday he and I will sign our own peace treaty, but for now we're like North and South Korea—we've got an armistice agreement. No hostilities. We're not supposed to anyway." Another pause. "That's good, right? Oh and don't worry, I haven't been lonely. Because besides Younger Uncle, I'm still in touch with my boys. Friends for life, brothers for life." I kiss my palm and pat the burial site. "I better get going. I miss you, Mom. I love you. I can't wait to see you soon."

I stand. I walk, no slouching.

37.

"Woah! What're you doing, Rocky?" Strike yells from the backseat of Younger Uncle's beat-up car. "We're going to sink!"

I sly smile to myself as I swerve onto the sand, stepping on the gas a little and taking a quick look in the rearview mirror. Strike smacks his palm against his forehead. Patch's eye is the size of one of the clams I dug up on this very beach yesterday, and that's big. I look at Braid who's sitting next to me. He's gripping the armrest so tight that the veins on the back of his hand are bulging.

My boys surprised me this morning. They showed up at Younger Uncle's doorstep with wide grins, intoxicating glee, and casual clothing.

"We were going to rent a car," Braid said, smoothing the wrinkles on his t-shirt. "That's what I wanted to do, but these bozos—"

"Yeah, us bozos," Strike interrupted, "we thought, why not make you pick our asses up at the dock?"

Patch rolled his eye, shook his head, then smiled.

Braid spoke up. "Luckily, the guy at the car rental—your younger uncle's friend, remember?—offered to drop us off."

"Come on in, bozos," I said. As soon as I shut the door, torrential rain decided we needed a little more indoor catch up time. When the weather finally cleared up an hour ago, we exploded out of the house ready to enjoy the sun.

"Relax, guys," I say. "This is Sagot Beach, a very special beach. The sand is packed so hard that people drive on it all the time. Even tour buses." I hold up a finger. "Think of me as your tour guide."

"I don't know..." Strike begins.

I make my voice all professional and say, "Gentlemen, this beautiful beach was even used as a landing strip for airplanes during the Korean War."

"You can't get away from war stuff here, can you?" Braid asks, letting go of the armrest.

I shake my head. "Not really." I drive a little further and park. "Let's walk?"

Strikes looks left, then right. "Yes, please!"

We hop out and stroll on the sand toward the golden setting sun.

Braid looks back and down, inspecting the sand for imprints of his steps, or rather the lack of imprints. "It's like a hard cement sidewalk," he says.

I nod. We walk further. The Yellow Sea laps at nature's sidewalk, leaving behind a shiny surface. The sun rays bounce off of it and blind us. I slip on my Ray-Bans, the boys use their hands as visors.

"Hey," I say, "thanks for coming."

Patch pats my shoulder and smiles big.

"Just so you know, this isn't goodbye or anything," Strike says. "I've always wanted to go to L.A. I mean it is the City of Angels. Hot angels."

Braid shakes his head. "Do you ever think about anything besides girls?"

"Nope," he says.

Braid scoffs, then looks at me. "But seriously, Rocky," he says. "We'll visit you, for sure. Maybe we should take a road trip to New York City or something."

"Sounds good." I'm glad I'm wearing my shades because I'm pretty sure my eyes are glistening. That's what a sudden layer of I-miss-my-brothers-already will do. I blink hard so there's no leakage. Then I say, "I can't believe you guys will get to meet my mom."

A round of nods.

We walk in the quiet loveliness of the deserted beach.

Braid speaks up. "I gave the envelope to Ha-na yesterday," he says.

"Thank you. Did she open it?"

"I don't know. She said she'd read it when she got home." He lights up a cig. So do Strike and Patch. Braid looks at me. "No smoke?" he asks.

I shake my head. "I quit," I say.

He takes a drag, exhales.

"So," I say, "where'd you meet Ha-na?"

"She insisted I meet her in the art classroom. She was finishing up a painting. Her teacher was there. I bet she wanted to make sure there was a witness in case I acted up."

"What else did she say?" I ask.

He exhales. "Nothing."

"Her painting, what was it?"

Braid's eyes widen. "It was incredible. I mean even Ryu Biho would've been impressed," he whispers. "Unconventional for sure. An edgy, modern self-portrait. Full length. Dark brown skin and thick, jet black hair all sharp, angular. The cuts on her arms were blood red. But she had this soft, Mona Lisa smile. And in the background, Seoul was burning. She was walking out of the flames like a badass."

"Damn!"

"Yeah," Braid says. "My amuteur description doesn't even do it justice. I asked her about it. You want to know what she said?"

I force a slow nod so that my giddy anticipation doesn't show itself. "Sure."

"She said it was her 'leaving hell on earth', and that she was going to 'leave hell on earth soon enough for real,'" Braid says. He continues in a taut voice. "It freaked me out when she said that. I was like shit, is she going to kill herself or something? I think she read my mind because the next thing she said was, 'Don't worry, I'm taking a trip.'"

"Did she say where or when?"

Braid shakes his head. "I tried to get it out of her, but she wouldn't tell me."

She's taking a trip.

38.

Younger Uncle's vintage Sansui record player spins the delicate vinyl like a black billowing dress. Pavarotti sinks his being into *Maria, Mari*, injecting full-blown passion into the veins of the room. I'm paralyzed, but in a good way, listening to how my esteemed tenor can't find peace because he wants to see her, talk to her...

I hang onto his voice, not wanting a cure for the longing. Maybe someday I'll even relate.

A quiet knock.

Rhomboids of morning sun dance to the melody, across the tats on my chest, down my shorts, to the hardwood floors.

Louder knock that shakes me from my reverie. Then three more.

Better than four.

I groan as I haul myself off the purposefully weathered chair Younger Uncle and I built yesterday out of reclaimed wood. Was Younger Uncle expecting anyone? He didn't mention it before he left. I throw on my t-shirt, get to the door. Swing it open. The bottom rail scrapes, I look down. The sweeper has come off. Mental note to fix it later. I thrust my hand into the unruly mop of hair shooting out of my head like soybean sprouts in Jeonju. I start to yawn, but in an instant my mouth slams shut.

That face. Sleeveless short romper. The scars…

Then a sweet voice. "I got your letter."

It's Ha-na!

She's fanning herself with an envelope. *My* envelope with the red wax seal, broken.

At first all I can do is gawk, the way those guys used to at my mom.

"Well, aren't you going to invite me in?" she asks in a mostly toneless voice, but I catch the slight tremor in it.

The muscles around my mouth decide to cooperate, they stretch into a slight smile. "Oh. Yeah," I mumble, stepping to the side. "Come on in."

My eyes canvass her S-line as she glides by. So crass, I know, but I'm only human. A better human since I got to the island.

I follow her to the miniscule living room.

She stops, her eyes fixed on the Sansui. "Pavarotti," she whispers. Her hand starts moving.

I'm speechless. My mind flashes to the school dining hall that day I made her eat my cig. Her waving hand…

She's staring at nothing. Tiny particles float in the sunlight that bathes her face. She starts gesturing with both hands.

I can't help but think of Claudio Abbado sculpting and shaping a Pavarotti performance at La Scala. I find my words. "One of my favorites," I say, unable to peel my gaze away from the smooth, dark skin of her conducting hands and her perfect French manicure.

"Mine too," she says without looking at me. She walks to the window and rests her hands on the sill.

That's when I notice the bit of blue paint on left hand.

A true artist, she carries her work with her. But how does she keep her fingernails so neat?

Sunny quadrangles illuminate her. The floral print on her romper seems to bloom, but her scars glare at me like faithful guard dogs who happen to be talking guard dogs. They growl, *She's not a black coolie! You're just a cruel brute! Hurt her again and you die!*

I almost put my hands up and back away, but I don't because I want to make peace. Then I scold my eyes for wanting another look at her legs. I hang my head in shameful repentance.

Awkward silence.

I break it with the only thing I can think of, a question. "Do you want some ginger tea?"

"Ok," she replies. She follows me to the kitchen.

I set a kettle to boil, then pluck a big piece of fresh ginger from the basket of fruits and vegetables. I peel it, grate it into a glass measuring cup, and add some honey.

Ha-na's standing next to me, close, so close that I can feel the heat from her body. My hand trembles a little, and I end up dropping the last spoonful of honey. Transparent gold oozes onto the counter. I wipe up the sticky mess.

"Your uncle has a nice place," she says.

I look up.

She's adjusting the messy bun near the top of her head. It wobbles a little. So do her dangly gold earrings. "So minimalist," she says with a blank expression.

"Yeah. My younger uncle prefers 'less stuff and more living,'" I say.

She nods.

The kettle whistles. I pour the hot water over the ginger and honey. The sharp almost lemony aroma floats through the house.

She closes her eyes and inhales. "Smells divine," she says.

"Younger Uncle got me into this brew. Better than the whiskey and makgeolli I used to drink like water."

"I bet your liver is happier."

I wonder if she's trying to joke around because even though her expression is flat there's a hint of sarcasm in her voice.

I nod, straining the tea into ceramic cups. Carefully I lift one cup with the fingertips of both my hands and offer it to her. "Please," I say with a little bow, the same way my mom used to do when she served my dad tea.

She receives the cup in both of her hands. She bows her head. "Thank you."

"Let's go sit," I suggest.

We return to the living room. She sits on the sofa, I take the chair. Pavarotti's singing *Tu, ca nun chiagne*. His emotions and something about the luminous natural light in the room make my mind wander to Naples. Not that I've ever been there, but I've seen plenty of photos in my dad's books. I imagine Ha-na and me at an outdoor cafe. A crisp, bright morning. In my head I whisper, "You don't cry, but you make me cry because I want you."

Do I?

She examines the amber liquid in her cup, then takes a sip. "Delicious," she whispers and looks up from her tea cup, gifts me with a full view of her beautiful face. It's a canvas today—red rouged cheeks, smokey eye makeup, and soft, pink lip gloss.

She's an angel.

I never noticed her wearing makeup before. Then again I never really noticed her before. Not until recently.

Maybe she wore makeup all along, or maybe she just started. Maybe she's wearing it today for me? And maybe she got her nails done for me? I draw my face back inside. *Shut up! Stop being so full of yourself!*

The angel parts her lips. "You were saying about your younger uncle, that he wants to do 'more living.' I guess that's why I'm here," she says.

I shift in place. "Oh?" I ask, straining to keep my voice and face even so I don't give away the fireworks exploding in my body. It hits me that it's never been this difficult for me to be a rock. What would my mom say? Especially about me talking to this half-Indian girl.

Ha-na retrieves the envelope from her pocket and lays it on the sofa next to her. "I read it," she says, flipping it over. She glances at me, her eyes shine like new black billiard balls. "Thank you," she says. She sips.

I can't breathe for a second as her last two words rack up and break in my head.

The record skips, and Pavarotti sings the same word over and over. We both look at the Sansui.

Ha-na gives me a half smile. "May I?" she asks.

I cock my head. "Be my guest," I say.

She cruises over and lifts the needle, lays it back down at the outer rim. *Torna a Surriento* starts. She looks over at me with a wide grin.

Warmth spills out of my heart, spreading thick through my body like the honey on the counter.

She plops onto the sofa. She takes two more sips of tea, then looks in the cup. "I think this just might be my new favorite tea," she says in English, with a British accent. She giggles, I think because she realizes what she said rhymed.

I sit up straight. "Do you want some more?" I ask.

She nods.

I hustle to the kitchen.

She joins me. "So, where's your younger uncle?" she asks. She leans against a wall and crosses her arms. "Is he doing 'more living?'" She smiles.

I finish peeling the ginger. "Yeah, I guess fishing counts as that."

"Well, the fish aren't too happy about that kind of more living," she says, then laughs.

I laugh, too. I finish grating the ginger. "So what are you doing this summer?" I ask as I add honey. This time, no mess.

She strokes her arm and smiles to herself. "An art internship in Los Angeles…"

39.

The steam rises in a little dance of twists and dips from the thick yellow-green tea in my ceramic cup. I inhale its fragrance deep into my lungs. It smells dewy fresh and earthy like morning grass. The first sip coats my tongue with a sweet and muddy taste that tumbles down my throat warm and soothing. "I like it," I say.

Younger Uncle smiles. He takes a sip. "Mmm," he says, "you brewed it perfect. This time I only had lotus leaf, but next time let's try to find the flower and root as well."

I nod. "A triple lotus tonic," I say.

He chuckles, then takes another sip. "A triple cleansing of all the alcohol and nicotine we've dumped into our bodies over the years."

I hold up my cup. "In that case, let me drink up," I say.

He laughs and sets his cup down. He lays one arm on the small table. "Your mom loves the triple mélange."

I half smile. *Maybe I can make it for her.* I take a slow sip.

"So, how did it go with Ha-na?"

I choke on my sip, all of a sudden I'm a tea kettle on a high flame because when I touch my cheek it's hot. That means it's red. I haven't opened my mouth, but it seems that my face has answered for me. *Thanks a lot.*

"That good, huh?" Younger Uncle says with a devilish gleam in his eye. "I'm intrigued. Do tell."

"I think she forgave me," I say.

"That's good news."

I don't say anything else.

"That's it?"

"Isn't that enough?"

He raises an eyebrow.

I open my mouth to say more, but change my mind and close it.

"Come on already." He drums his fingers on the table.

One, two, three. One, two, three. One, two, three.

I put my palms up. "Ok, ok," I say. "I can't believe she forgave me. I think it takes a huge heart to do that." I pause and drop my eyes. "Especially after the awful things I've done to her." I mumble. "I guess she's the second person with a huge heart I know. Mom's the first. You said it yourself, Mom loved Dad. She was always faithful to him. Even after what he put her through."

He nods. "She still loves him, even though she knew she had to get away from him," Younger Uncle says. "She says there is good in him... somewhere."

I look up and try to smile.

"Anyway, tell me more about what Ha-na said."

I tuck my chin, smiling to myself. Then I lift my eyes only. "She's going to L.A. this summer, an internship at the Getty. She's an incredible artist, you know."

He sits back and crosses his arms. "Oh boy."

"What?"

"L.A., huh?"

"Yeah."

"What an interesting coincidence."

"It's no big deal."

"No big deal," he says with a straight face. "If you say so."

"I do say so," I snap. Nothing else about Ha-na is going to escape these lips!

Unfortunately a second later the wires snap and my mouth flies open. "It's a huge deal, ok?! I can't stop thinking about her. She's smart and kind and sweet and gorgeous!"

Younger Uncle nods. "Now we're getting somewhere." He leans forward and clasps his hands on the table.

"I feel all weird inside," I say, leaving out the part about my gochu of course. Then I let out a soft breath. "I don't know what to do. I mean how wrong is it that a bully likes his victim? That's totally messed up, isn't it?"

Younger Uncle takes a sip. He steeples his fingers. "Unusual, maybe. But I wouldn't say totally messed up. It seems to me that you've changed."

I'm trying.

I raise one eyebrow and give a slow stroke to my sideburn. Deep down, I guess I'm not convinced I deserve to even think about her, let alone like her, with everything I've done.

Younger Uncle scoots his chair in. "Listen, change is possible. Living proof right here," he says pointing his thumb at himself. Then he points at me with his chin. "You aren't a bully anymore. And she's not your victim anymore."

"So what should I do?"

"You have to be honest with yourself and with Ha-na. That's one of the secrets to more living."

"Maybe I can be honest with myself, but with Ha-na...I don't know. I mean all that bullying can't be erased just like that, even if she forgave me. It seems totally out of line and conceited of me to hope that she'd like me back."

Younger Uncle shakes his head. "I don't think it's either. In fact, you won't go wrong if you get out of your head and focus on being honest. You're not hurting her anymore, you've apologized profusely, and she forgave you. So you should try to be honest from here on out. It's the right thing to do." He pauses for a sip. "Now I'm not saying you should forget what you've done. Don't ever forget the pain you put her through." He pushes up his sleeves, brushes his tiger and dragon. "I'll never forget what I did. And that helps me to do the right thing now." He pulls his sleeves back down. "Every day I remind myself what I've done. Every day I remind myself what I want to do instead."

"What if she laughs in my face?"

"Maybe she will, but being honest is not about predicting or controlling the other person's reaction. It's about being your true self. It's about being truthful in your deeds and words."

"I guess."

"Look, I told your mom the truth—that I loved her but not just as a sister-in-law. She told me her truth—that she loved me like a brother, not like a lover. Of course that crushed me. But the honesty we shared made us closer. If we weren't that close, she might not have told me about what your dad did to her. She might not have reached out to me on that brutal night. I'm grateful she turned to me. I'm grateful she let me help her." He takes a sip. "I wouldn't trade that for anything."

"But the woman you love isn't here. You must be lonely," I whisper.

"It's true your mom's not here and that when you leave I will be alone in this house. But I'm not lonely. I'm living how I want. I chose not to be a minister like my dad. I changed my mind about being a gang boss like my brothers. I've figured out what I want, what I stand for. I have some good friends, and your mom is one of them. I also have you. Even when neither of you are here." He pauses to thump his chest once, "You're both in here."

I sit straighter as Younger Uncle's words reassure me. *I'm not lonely. I've got my boys, my mom, and Younger Uncle. And I've made peace with Hana. Things are ok right now. In fact, things are good right now, very good.*

Dusk tosses muted light through the windows, and I feel lighter. I take another sip, the tea tastes even better. I look at Younger Uncle. "Thank you," I say with a slight head bow.

40.

I'm waiting to board my flight here at Incheon International Airport. I'm a caged tiger, and I want to pace. But I can't move, not a muscle. A drop of sweat rolls down my forehead, I want to brush it. Can't.

More drops percolate out of my skin to form what I feel certain is an unattractive sheen on my face, and I want to wipe it. Can't. A thousand needles prick me, suddenly I'm sweating all over. I want to peel off my sweater and shirt underneath. Can't. I want to walk. Can't. I want to pull out my pocket watch, check the time…

Can't do anything. Can't risk it. Because it feels like if I give in to any of my urges, something bad will happen. The worst something bad—I won't get to see Mom. As crazy as all that sounds when I really think about it, I'm not willing to take any chances. So I will remain a statue with my arms crossed and my back and one foot propped against this thick, wide support column.

I do the only thing I can do—take in the scene before my unmoving eyes. The airport is a swarming ant colony with its mix of faces and bodies scurrying in organized chaos. I count the people wearing black coats. When I get to fifty, I feel a little better so I stop counting.

There are many different looking, different sounding, and differently dressed people here. Way more than on the streets of Seoul or on the island. And with their half smiles or full grins they all seem happy. Happy to travel? Probably. I wonder where they're all going. Visiting family? Returning home? Going on vacation? Searching for adventure in some far off land?

Searching...

My insides squirm.

Mom.

Don't jinx it! Think about something else!

So I invent a game to pass the time until boarding the plane can free me from my state of purposeful immobility. I call it *What Is This Traveler Searching For?*

A wizened old man is in my line of sight. He's hunched over the trash can dressed in an airport janitor's uniform, so he's not traveling. He might be one of the poorer forgotten generation that really should be retired. Younger Uncle was telling me about that, it makes me so sad. I examine his wrinkled face. Even though he's working here, I'm sure he's still searching. My guess—it's for the basics of life, money, food, and shelter.

Then there's the American who's more than a head higher than the tallest person in his vicinity. Fancy business suit, brown leather attaché case, and obnoxious slicked-to-the-side blond hair. He's walking and talking on his cell, laughing way too loud, and eyeing all the pretty young Korean girls. This guy reminds me of my dad. And I take a guess that he's searching for the same thing as my dad—more. More money. More power. More sex. More everything.

My stomach churns, and I burp a silent burp. It leaves a bitter taste in my mouth. I stare off into the crowd, only I'm not really seeing anything.

Until I see her.

A riot breaks out in my body.

I stare at this girl.

A stunning girl.

Dark with familiar features.

Ha-na!

Now there's a full on revolution inside as my body defies my mind's orders to remain still. I push myself off the wall...

She's walking this way, a backpack slung over her shoulder. My eyes don't give me a choice—they insist on checking her out. Tight jeans. Hoodie. Hair in a high, loose ponytail. Her face sans makeup...*an angel*.

Wait a second.

My mom's an angel, but Ha-na...she's a modern, super-hot Mona Lisa with serious flavor. I imagine her walking towards me with Seoul burning in the background. A badass. I smile inside.

She looks down at her boarding pass, then checks the gate signs on her left and right. She keeps walking.

Is she going to L.A. today?

We never actually exchanged all our travel details.

She stops again, this time in front of my gate and glances at the sign.

Then she slips her boarding pass into her pocket and proceeds in. She sits down.

Could she really be on this flight?

I rub my clammy palms on my jeans and count to three before I let myself saunter over to her, though what I really want to do is run.

There's an empty seat next to her, and I crash down in it, let out a big breath before I say, "Looks like a full flight, no?"

She turns her head to me and smiles a warm smile.

My pits feel like the Banpo Bridge water fountain show. "So, you're on this flight?"

She nods.

I facepalm and groan inside. On the outside all I do is mumble, "Right."

Her face softens. She says, "You must be thrilled. I mean seeing your mom for the first time in ten years."

I nod.

"I'm happy for you."

"Thanks...so...when do you start at the Getty?"

Her eyes burst like a dazzling sunrise over the Han. "Next week."

"You're not *that* excited, are you?"

She giggles. "No. Only a tad...pleased."

I smile. "I never thought we'd be on the same flight."

She nods. "I know. I was supposed to be on an earlier flight, but it got cancelled. Engine problems they said. So they put me on this one." She pulls off her scrunchie and slides it onto her wrist. "What a coincidence," she says, redoing her ponytail in the blink of an eye.

I picture Younger Uncle. *What an interesting coincidence.*

My heart beats faster. "Yeah." I try to keep my voice matter-of-fact. "How is it that we end up running into each other all the time?"

She cocks her head. "I don't know," she says.

The silence that follows is uncomfortable for me. I fidget.

Ha-na seems unphased as she stares at the overhead TV monitor. The news guy is talking about some factory strike. She looks at me, resting her head on her hand. "Maybe," she says, "life is trying to tell us something."

"Life is trying to tell us something..." I say under my breath.

I picture Younger Uncle again.

Don't ever forget the pain you put her through.

Check that box. A million times over.

...you should try to be honest from here on out. It's the right thing to do.

Well, I've been honest in my apology. It was difficult but it was obviously the right thing to do. Telling her what else I feel, that seems impossible. Plus I'm still not one hundred percent sure it's the right thing to do.

A gentle touch. I look. Ha-na's hand is on my shoulder.

"Rocky?" she asks, "are you ok?"

I nod. "I was just thinking about what you said." I look into her eyes. "You're right, life is trying to tell us something." Then I drop my eyes. "Well, tell me something," I whisper.

"What?"

"I-I..." I tap the floor three times, then I try again. "I-I..." I can't do it.

I glance at Ha-na, her brow is furrowed. I exhale long and slow, wishing I hadn't quit smoking. I can't be honest with all my feelings just yet so I ask her a question instead. "What do you think life is trying to tell you?"

She balances her chin on the back of her hand and looks at me with kind eyes. "Maybe seeing you is life's way of reminding me that I can get through anything."

I give her a half smile. Only half because inside I'm a little disappointed. I don't want her to just get *through* me, but then I nod because what she said makes sense, and I'm just being full of myself for wanting more.

We sit quietly for a bit. It's not an uncomfortable silence.

Ha-na lifts her backpack onto her lap and searches through the front pocket until she finds what she's looking for—her phone. Her earbuds are already plugged in. She untangles the long cord and hands me one side.

I insert the earbud.

She inserts the other, then scrolls through her phone playlist. "Close your eyes," she says.

I do.

A powerful voice elicits an automatic tingle in my spine.

It's Pavarotti. *Nessun Dorma.*

Warmth spreads through my body.

I end up lost in some sunny Italian village...

Pavarotti's gorgeous tenor sound and robust emotions build up. I'm walking through an endless vineyard, hand in hand with a beautiful half-

Indian, half-Korean girl. I stop to gaze into her eyes. *I love you,* I say. Then my opera hero belts out different lyrics, ones I've written.

> *Foe is now friend.*
> *I wish someday a girlfriend.*
> *Seeing Mom this weekend.*
> *New life just around the bend.*
> *More happiness than I can comprehend.*

41.

When the captain announces the plane's descent into LAX, I push the window shade up. The wing slices through dense clouds, and somewhere in the distance a soft morning light makes the white puffs gleam like snow. I can't see the city yet, but I can imagine…

The city of angels. *My angel.* I swallow hard to unplug my clogged ears, then I close my eyes. Mom's voice.

My little Yi Kyung-seok…

I whisper, "Mom."

She strokes my cheek. My little Yi Kyung-seok. My little Rocky…

I touch my cheek with my jittery hand. I've longed for her all these years, but no one really knew how much—the secret yearning was buried deep in the spongy parts of my bones, quietly boomeranging in the crevices. Yet the secret was too big to remain completely contained and bits of it leaked out. A slow, continuous leak that turned into a chill. It made me cold-blooded, made me do unspeakable things.

Mom looks into my eyes. Your eyes are icy cold black like your dad's…

I shake my head three times. *No! I'm nothing like Dad! I'm going to* show you, Mom. Rub my eyes. *I've been thawing out, I'm not icy cold. I'm not a stone-cold killer like Dad. I'm not a rock.*

My eyelids rip apart. *Relax!*

I fiddle with the latch of the tray table. Then I peek through the seats, two rows up. Ha-na's head is slumped to the right, almost resting on the shoulder of the older woman next to her. Sleeping, it seems. I try to get a look at her arms, but I can't see them.

I'm not a bully.

My heart pounds like a drummer on a traditional Korean drum.

The plane hits the tarmac and lurches forward. I grip my armrests as my new reality grips me—Mom's a few minutes away.

She strokes my cheek. My little Yi Kyung-seok. My little Roc—

No, Mom. I'm not Rocky. *You* named me Kyung-seok.

Yi Kyung-seok. That's who I am.

I smile a satisfied smile inside.

I check between the seats, Ha-na's up. She looks over her shoulder. Her hair is down, an avalanche of lustrous black curls. Her onyx eyes shine, coaxing my lips into an outside smile. She smiles back.

The plane crawls to the gate, and the brief time it takes for the doors to open feel like forever. And a day. Finally we're allowed to deplane. I rocket out of my seat. Though I didn't sleep much on the flight, I'm charged like I just chugged a Bacchus-F. No, three of them.

Ha-na's waiting for me inside the terminal, leaning against the wall with one hand on her hip. When she sees me, she grabs her backpack off the floor and hoists it onto her shoulder.

I get within earshot.

"I thought you'd be running," she says with one eyebrow raised.

I shake my head and chuckle. "No. I'm a cool guy. Always a cool guy," I say. I loud exhale, then whisper, "It's a curse."

She fake frowns. "Whatever. Let's go, Rocky." She waves her hand.

Rocky.

I flinch, but she doesn't notice. I stare ahead of me as we walk towards passport control. I say, "Maybe you can call me Kyung-seok now. You know, instead of Rocky."

She cranks her head to me. "Why? What's wrong with Rocky?"

I adjust my backpack and stuff my hands in my pockets. "Well, Rocky is the nickname my mom gave me when I was kid and seeing as I'm older now and you know..." I pause.

"What?"

"Well, I'm not a bully anymore. And I'm trying not to be a horrible excuse of a human being. I'm trying to be a different person. Maybe it's a good thing to have a different name. Not my old boss name. Besides, Kyung-seok is my real name."

"Kyung-seok," she whispers to herself. She looks at me and smiles. "Kyung-seok it is."

"Thanks," I say. I like how my real name sounds. Or, is it that I like that she's saying it? There's a new spring in my step as we walk.

We fall into line at passport control. I study the other travelers. So many diverse faces. I listen to the unique languages, I count at least five I've never heard. I look at Ha-na. I wonder if she'll meet my mom today.

It hits me again. *She's not missing or dead.*

I tap Ha-na's shoulder.

"Yes, Kyung-seok?" she asks.

"Who's picking you up?"

"My aunt. My 'crazy' aunt," she says making air quotes. "My dad's sister. The one who's a 'free spirit' as he says. As if that's a bad thing, right?" She shrugs, shaking her head. Then she says, "Who's—" She cuts herself off, giggles.

"What?" I ask.

She tilts her head and half smiles. "I was just about to ask who's picking you up."

"My mo—."

"Yeah," she says nodding.

"Next in line," a customs officer calls.

"See you on the other side," Ha-na whispers before stepping forward.

We get through quick and easy and then walk towards baggage claim.

"Let's step on it," Ha-na says.

A hard nod. "Let's."

We hustle the rest of the way. Many of the passengers are already poised around the slow-moving carousel when we get there. Ha-na and I find a place to stand at the far end, between the wall and the tallest man I've ever seen.

"My bag's red. What color is yours?" Ha-na asks.

"Black. But it's got a yellow belt," I say. *Yellow is Mom's favorite color.*

I count the black bags as they pass like plates of seaweed-wrapped sushi on a conveyor belt.

"There's mine," Ha-na says, extending her arm to grab it.

I gently push her arm down. "Please. Let me." I wrap my fingers around the handle and hoist it. It weighs more than I expect. I set it down next to her. "What the heck's in here? Bars of gold?"

"Ha! You, Kyung-seok, obviously aren't an artist. If you were, you'd know art supplies can be heavy." She lowers her eyes and plays with her name tag. The thin metal chain twists around the bag's handle. "Actually, I need all my stuff because I'm not going back to Seoul," she whispers.

Confusion washes over my face leaving me stuck with cow eyes and a partial frown. But then it all computes. ...*I'll be moving onto bigger and better things than all of you pathetic bully losers with nothing better to do than kick people when they're down.* Maybe she's decided not to wait until finishing the last year of school in Seoul before starting her new life.

I'm about to tell her that I'm not going back either.

"Is that your bag?" she asks pointing.

I grab it from the carousel.

"Well, then," she says. She sweeps her arm in front of her, all dramatic. "After you."

"No," I say. I sweep my arm in front of me and bow. "After you. I insist."

"Thanks," she says.

We cruise towards customs. When we get to the front of the line, I let Ha-na go first.

"See you on the other side again," she whispers.

After our bags are searched and officially cleared, we regroup under a sign that points the way to the exit. We exchange smiles and start to walk.

Suddenly I wish I was Rocky again. Or better yet, a real rock. Because then maybe I wouldn't be consumed by this overwhelming urge to reveal my truth to her.

Tell her!

"Wait, Ha-na," I say.

She stops and turns to face me. "What's up?"

"I-I have to tell you something."

"What?"

I fork my fingers through my hair.

"What is it, Kyung-seok?"

"You said you're not going back to Seoul. Well, I'm not going back either. I'm going to live with my mom. I was just thinking…" I pause, staring at my feet.

"What?"

I force myself to look at her.

"The thing is, both of us are going to be in L.A."

You pretty much said that already, idiot!

She nods.

I keep going. "Maybe we should…" I pause, swallow hard.

She tips her head to one side and waits.

"I…" I stare at her.

Her eyebrows rise. "You…"

I like you!

But that's not what comes out of my mouth. I end up blurting, "We should keep in touch!"

Her face doesn't change, but she also doesn't say anything.

At least she doesn't seem totally repulsed.

Then it seems like we're stuck in an awkward eternity in which all I can do is cringe inside. I want to suck my words back in. I want to deny it, say I was just joking. But I can't move my lips. It takes everything in me to get my mouth to work again. "I'm sorry," I say. I shift in place and groan. "I realize keeping in touch with your former bully is probably the last thing you want to do. You don't have to—"

She lays her hand on my shoulder. "Kyung-seok," she says, "I want to keep in touch with you too. I was planning on it." She pulls out her cell and holds it up. "You've got Line, right?"

I nod.

"Me too. Message me anytime. And send me your new number when you get it. I'll do the same."

I pump my arms and jump for joy, but only on the inside.

"Don't be a stranger," she whispers, twirling her hair, then tucking it behind her ear.

My heart goes kablooey, but I keep myself in check. "I won't," I say, dropping my head and smiling. When I look back at her, she's smiling too.

"Shall we?" she asks, pointing to the exit with her chin.

"Yes." I follow her as she weaves through the people towards the large sliding glass doors leading to the street. Without warning, she stops dead in her tracks. I almost run into her but catch myself just in time, then step beside her. I see what she sees, an Indian woman maybe in her forties with a regal face, long, curly black hair flowing over her shoulders, and a colorful boho-chic short dress with brown leather boots. I look at Ha-na, her eyes are wet, and her lip is quivering.

"Your aunt?" I ask.

She nods. She turns to me and says in a soft voice, "Later, Kyung-seok, not goodbye." She bows.

I bow.

We look at each other for a second before she extends her arms for a hug, I think, but something makes her change her mind. Her arms drop, so does her jaw, and her eyes are glued behind me. Then only her lips move. "Kyung-seok, I think I see an angel. Is that your..."

An angel...

The world around me stops. My eyes are scanning, searching.

I see her.

An angel. My angel.

She looks the same as I remember. Just like in the old wedding photo. A lovely, noble Korean woman. Her shiny black hair is in a sleek, low bun at her nape. Her high symmetrical cheekbones are brushed a perfect deep rose, and her lips are painted red, blood red. *The country's most promising ingénue. A true rising star. Gangster boss' wife. Gil Bo-Young.*

My mom.

My heart skips a beat, then seems to come to a standstill, like my face and my entire being. I'm suspended between disbelief and joy, and I can't do anything. I can't smile. I can't cry. I can't tap. Seconds pass. Or is it minutes? Hours? My head battles with itself. *Is she a photo? A memory? Or is she real?*

Her eyes find mine, and she throws her hands up to cup her mouth. Her face scrunches a little. She approaches me, slow, like maybe she thinks I'm an apparition or a dream.

I see the tears falling freely from her eyes. She's smiling at me the way she did all those years ago. Now she standing in front of me.

She's real.

I count her laugh lines. Three on either side of each eye. Just the right number.

She extends her shaky hands up to cradle my face, crying hard but quiet. One of her hands slides to the back of my head, caresses it.

My eyes slowly fill with tears.

"My little Kyung-seok, not so little anymore," she whispers.

Suddenly my body convulses and then not just my eyes, but my whole body, cries for the ten years I've missed with her.

She holds my face and wipes my tears with her thumbs. She reaches into her purse and brings out a handkerchief with a stitched border.

Green, single thread…

She dabs my cheeks. "Here, use this. I made it for you."

I take the soft white cloth and blot my face. I flip it over, and that's when I see the willow tree, the same as the one she stitched on Dad's handkerchief. I pull his out of my pocket to show her.

She takes it and holds it to her heart. "So now you have two," she whispers.

I nod.

"I'm sorry for everything," she says. She dries her face with Dad's handkerchief. "I'm here now," she whispers. She wraps her arms around me and presses her cheek on my chest because that's how much taller I am than her. She squeezes me in the tightest bear hug. "I've missed you so much, Kyung-seok."

I lift one arm up, drape it around her, then the other. I don't want to let go. I don't want her to let go. I try to think of what to say, but my brain can't formulate thoughts. Even if it could, my vocal cords and mouth aren't functioning anyway.

Ever so gently she pulls away. She takes my hands in hers. More tears fall from our eyes, but neither of us wipes them away.

"So many years," she whispers. She looks at my hands, strokes my dragon tat, then my tiger tat. "We've got each other now. We're safe," she says.

"Mom," I say in a wobbly voice. "I-I..."

She shakes her head and smiles. "It's ok," she says. "We've got time. All the time in the world. I'll make it up to you. I promise." She touches my cheek, then whispers, "Did you eat?"

I smile inside, and out, because that question from my mom sounds like beautiful music to my ears. I tap my thigh once, twice, but make myself resist the third. My heart speeds up, and it's harder to breath. That's how difficult it is not to tap the lucky third time. But I endure because it's time for a change. A good change. And I'm hopeful—ready—for my new life.

New life just around the bend.

More happiness than I can comprehend.

ACKNOWLEDGMENTS

I am forever grateful to the people who helped me navigate my *Bloody Seoul* journey.

My deepest thanks and bow to the following people:

Everyone at Cinco Puntos Press for their faith in my stories.

Lee Byrd for your vision and wise and straight-up editing. You're still always right!

J.L. Powers for your multiple readings and insightful comments that helped me see things I couldn't.

Bobby Byrd, John Byrd, Jill Bell, and Mary Fountaine for the behind-the-scenes work that made this book a reality.

Gregory Lee and Hyunjin Han for the cultural guidance that allowed me to keep this book more real than I could've otherwise.

Annis Lee Adams, John Manaligod, and Jaclyn Marie Brown for offering fresh perspectives that helped me shape the book.

Zeke Peña for the incredible cover art that, for a third time, left me speechless, jaw dropped.

James Manaligod, Maya Manaligod, Joaquin Manaligod, and Hansa Patel. My angels.

SONIA PATEL knows teenagers inside and out. As a child and adolescent psychiatrist, trained at Stanford University and the University of Hawaii, she has spent over fifteen years listening to and understanding the psyche of teenagers from all walks of life. She chose South Korea as the setting for her third YA novel, *Bloody Seoul*, because of her extensive treatment experience with Korean and Korean American teens on Oahu (and her love for the Korean gangster film genre).

As a writer, Sonia is passionate about giving voice to the underrepresented youth she treats. Her YA debut featuring a Gujarati-Indian American teen, *Rani Patel In Full Effect*, was a finalist for the Morris Award and was listed on YALSA's Best Fiction for Young Adults and Kirkus' Reviews Best Teen Books of 2016. Her second YA novel, with a Gujarati-Indian trans boy and a mixed ethnicity girl, *Jaya and Rasa: A Love Story*, was selected for the 2019 In the Margins Book Award Recommended Fiction Book List. She's also been a teenage girl herself, growing up on Moloka'i as a first generation Gujarati-American.